# JACKMAN'S WOLF

Center Point
Large Print

Also by Ray Hogan and available from
Center Point Large Print:

*Panhandle Gunman*
*The Steel Angel*
*Conger's Woman*
*Against the Law*
*Texas Flat*
*The Glory Trail*
*Law Comes to Lawless*

**This Large Print Book carries the
Seal of Approval of N.A.V.H.**

# JACKMAN'S WOLF

## Ray Hogan

CENTER POINT LARGE PRINT
THORNDIKE, MAINE

This Center Point Large Print edition
is published in the year 2019 by arrangement with
Golden West Literary Agency.

First US edition: Doubleday
First UK edition: Curley

The text of this Large Print edition is unabridged.
In other aspects, this book may vary
from the original edition.
Printed in the United States of America
on permanent paper.
Set in 16-point Times New Roman type.

ISBN: 978-1-64358-136-1 (hardcover)
ISBN: 978-1-64358-140-8 (paperback)

Library of Congress Cataloging-in-Publication Data

Names: Hogan, Ray, 1908-1998, author.
Title: Jackman's wolf / Ray Hogan.
Description: Center Point Large Print edition. | Thorndike, Maine :
    Center Point Large Print, 2019.
Identifiers: LCCN 2018059299| ISBN 9781643581361 (hardcover :
    alk. paper) | ISBN 9781643581408 (paperback : alk. paper)
Subjects: LCSH: Ranchers. | Ranch life. | Western stories. |
    Large type books.
Classification: LCC PS3558.O3473 J3 2019 | DDC 813/.54—dc23
LC record available at https://lccn.loc.gov/2018059299

*To my wife, Lois . . . for without her*
*There would be nothing*

# CHAPTER ONE

He was still alive, which was more than could be said for his horse, Matt Rusk realized, stirring painfully on the rock-studded ground at the foot of the bluff; one moment he was riding along the trail—the next he was plunging downward in a choking cloud of red clay dust.

He sat up slowly, feeling the sun's driving heat beating against him, the crawling of sweat upon his skin, the stinging and smarting of a dozen scratches and abrasions, and glanced around. The sorrel had ceased his thrashing, now lay quiet in the wedge of rocks into which he'd fallen, neck twisted and folded back under his body.

Rusk rubbed at his head. A haze was drifting about in his brain, and he was having difficulty focusing his eyes, but all was clearing gradually. After a few moments he raised his glance to the rim of the butte, a good forty feet above . . . It had been one hell of a fall, he decided.

The layers of red dust continued to hang in the motionless air of the canyon, and now that the racket and confusion the spill had created was over, insects were resuming their noisy clacking and small forms of wild life began to stir . . . With little interest Matt Rusk watched a tan and white gopher pop out on a nearby ledge, race along its rim for a short distance, and then disappear into a hole.

He wiped at his mouth, his eyes. He just couldn't sit there. Again he looked up to the edge of the butte. That first drop, when the rain loosened earth had given way under the sorrel, hadn't been too bad; it was the second ledge, collapsing under the sudden, falling weight of the gelding that had done the damage.

Damage . . . Rusk rolled the word about in his mind dully until it finally registered. Slowly then he pulled his six-foot frame upright. He was aching and throbbing in several locations but there was no sharp, stabbing pain that would indicate a broken bone. Brushing again at the dust caked on his sweaty face, he made his way uncertainly over the uneven ground to the declivity in which the dead horse lay.

A damp circle on the surface of the porous sandstone flashed a message to him. *Goddammit,* he thought and hunched beside the body of the animal. His canteen had been caught underneath, had burst, and all its contents lost.

Matt Rusk settled back on his heels, stared at his gloved hands, a look of patient resignation on his hard-cornered features. A big man, thick shouldered and muscular, he was running now to gauntness, tribute to the aimless way of life he'd acquired since pulling up stakes in Montana.

Lifting his head, he studied the surrounding country with moody indifference.

He was in a strange land—somewhere east of the Sangre de Cristo Mountains, he knew that much, and he was in the outcroppings of a second, much smaller range he'd heard called the Sagebrush Hills. "Pretty damn good hills," he muttered, letting his gaze run up the rugged brush- and rock-strewn slopes lifting steeply before him . . . No timber, hardly any growth except scrubby weeds. That meant there'd be no water.

Turning, he looked to the west, to the hazy blue outlines of the towering Sangre de Cristos. Towns, people in that direction—but they'd be too far. Best he keep bearing east just as he'd been doing when the trail caved in under him. He'd seen smoke in the sky somewhere beyond the Sagebrushes; that meant a ranch, or possibly even a small town.

Once more he swept the rough slopes of the hills before him, sighed, and dropped to his knees beside the sorrel. Taking the headstall in his hands, he pulled until he had straightened out the animal's broken neck, then removed the bridle.

Tossing it aside, he put his attention to the saddle cinch, began to work at the strap and buckle. High overhead great, gliding shadows were beginning to appear, circling slowly, maintaining a careful distance. They'd not come, he knew, until he was gone and there were no signs of life around the horse.

He got the cinch free, laid it back, and grasping the saddle by the fork, attempted to pull it clear. It slipped part way, hung as a stirrup caught under the sorrel's belly, wedged tight. Matt worked doggedly at it under the blazing sun for a half hour, gave it up.

There was nothing around stout enough to pry with, and although a powerful man, he simply hadn't the strength to move the sorrel's dead weight . . . The hell with it. The hull was old, so was the bridle and everything else he had; he could replace the lot for a double-eagle . . . The canteen was all that had value—and it only because it had contained water. Now it was worthless, too. He shrugged wearily. The hell with all of it—the whole kit and kaboodle. None of it was worth any effort.

Knuckling sweat from his eyes, he stared at the long slopes again. Gray rock shining dully in the sun—so damned hot a man could render sowbelly on the ledges. Heat waves shimmered everywhere; snakeweed, prickly pear, ragged flowered groundsel, here and there a faded gray juniper . . . One hell of a place to be caught afoot.

The smoke again, a faint streamer trickling up into the bright, steel-blue arch of the cloudless sky. How far? Two miles—five—ten, maybe.

No way of telling. Only one thing was certain—it came from beyond the Sagebrush Hills.

The corners of Rusk's mouth pulled down into a bleak, mirthless smile. His shoulders bunched, his body swayed forward and he started up the slope. In two strides he was down on hands and knees, cursing steadily, morosely. He fought himself to an upright position, plunged on.

If he could make it over this hell of rock and scorched weeds with no water and the heat hovering somewhere around a hundred degrees, he just might reach the source of that smoke . . . If he didn't—well, no man could expect to live forever.

April Jackman brushed a stray wisp of dark hair from her eyes, brushed also at the sweat collected along the ridge of her nose, and resumed the chore of loosening soil around the tomato plants with the hoe. It was too hot to be working in the garden, but the job had to be done; ordinarily she would have begun earlier but Clint, her young brother, had gotten a late start for town that morning, and it had thrown her behind with everything.

It wasn't like the old days—five years ago, or even three. Her father had been alive then and the Jackman Lazy J ranch was a good, going concern with hired hands aplenty to do things like tending the family vegetable plot.

But Amos Jackman's death at the hands of an unknown killer had changed everything. In no time at all, it seemed, most of the cattle that remained after the market drive that spring were gone, what few dollars had been on hand were spent, and when the prospects of no wages forthcoming had become apparent to the hired help, they also vanished.

Now there was just Clint and herself, and maybe two hundred steers living in the middle of an eighty thousand acre ranch . . . Living . . . April's upper lip curled wryly at the word. Existing was more like it—and to what end? What was the future? Were she and Clint just going to stay there, living a hand-to-mouth, day-to-day sort of life until doomsday? Was there nothing other than that to look forward to?

Clint had dreams of rebuilding the ranch, of getting more cattle and making the Lazy J brand known again among stock growers and buyers; but Clint was only a boy with a boy's grand dreams, and he'd been far too young to accept the load that had settled upon his shoulders when their father had died in that ambush.

Clint didn't realize, or perhaps he did and didn't let on, that it took money to do all the things he planned to one day accomplish—money and help, and they had neither and no prospects of obtaining them.

The fact was, matters were sliding the other

way. Their small herd was being slowly and systematically rustled, two or three head at a time. And they had already signed over twenty beeves to John Larkin at the general store in Cabezo to pay for supplies—items like coffee, flour, sugar, other articles she couldn't grow in her garden.

Some day, between the rustling and the bartering, they'd simply run out of cattle to pledge John Larkin, and that would be the end of the Jackman ranch. Things would simply come to a standstill, and they'd be forced to accept Frank Sutter's offer to buy—a ridiculous figure that amounted to less than twenty cents on the dollar insofar as the true value of the property was concerned—and let him take over what he'd been after for so many years—the Lazy J.

He had already made a move along such lines. Clint had spotted about five hundred head of Sutter cattle on their north range over a month ago. Clint was all for riding straight to Sutter's, demand the stock be moved off, but she had talked him out of it.

It would have done no good. Sutter would have just laughed in their faces, and the punchers would have had something new to hooraw Clint about when they caught him in town. April couldn't see that it really mattered much, anyway, their using the north range. The only part of the ranch they had need of was the south meadow which was more than ample for their small herd.

And she would rather give in to Sutter's encroachment, if you wanted the bald truth, than chance creating an incident wherein Clint might get hurt . . . She'd not soon forget the way their father died—a bullet reaching out of the shadows, tearing into his back, ripping the life from his body.

He'd been to a meeting of ranchers, one being held that particular time at Frank Sutter's, intended to ride on into town and bank the money he'd brought back after settling up at the end of the spring cattle drive, when the gathering was over. Nothing particular had occurred at the meeting—no argument, not even any hasty words, according to those who had been there.

But on the way into the settlement, some time later, Amos Jackman had been ambushed and robbed. There had been a token investigation by the town marshal, Avery Kingstreet, but nothing had come of it.

"Some drifter—outlaw," he had said to April and Clint. "Looking for a few dollars."

"A few!" she had echoed. "Papa was carrying every cent we had—almost. Over four thousand dollars. Without it we're broke."

The lawman had wagged his head, expressed his regret. "These things do happen, and I'm mighty sorry they've happened to you . . . I'll keep watching out, doing what I can to track down the killer."

That was the last of it so far as Avery Kingstreet was concerned, and they never heard from him again on the matter. Clint was convinced that Frank Sutter, or at least someone in his hire, had committed the crime—and for very obvious reasons. Only two ranches lay in the lush valley between the Sagebrush Hills and the Bitter Creek Trail: Sutter's and Jackman's.

Sutter, with over two hundred thousand acres already at his disposal, had tried several times to buy out his adjoining neighbor, add that eighty thousand acres spread to his holdings. He would then own the entire valley, from the Barranca Country, as the deep-gashed area to the north was called, to Skull Flats, with its wide spread tangle of brakes in the south.

But Amos Jackman had refused each offer, being content. The Lazy J was doing well; he owed nothing, there were a few dollars in the bank, and he had a fine, healthy herd. He could look forward to turning a profitable ranch over to his son, or to his daughter if she hadn't married and had a man and a place of her own, in a few years, spend his declining days taking it easy.

A bullet had cut short his plans—a bullet no one would ever convince young Clint Jackman had come from any gun except one directed by Frank Sutter. April had her beliefs, too, but she kept them to herself, never openly agreeing with Clint and his convictions for fear of encouraging him, inducing him to make a rash statement or possibly a wrong move; their father had been murdered—she'd not let the same thing happen to her brother.

It wasn't much of a future to look forward to—just sit there, exist while Sutter, like some irresistible blight moved in gradually and consumed the ranch. But at least there'd be no more killing—and Sutter would pay something; it might be less than he'd offered at the start, but it would be something.

And Clint would still be alive. That was what counted . . . Three more years, four at the most; that was all she asked of this pointless, drudging endurance, and then Clint will have matured, lost his boyish indignation and impulsiveness that could cost so dearly now if permitted to run rampant, and she'd have no need to worry over him any longer.

He would see the reason in what she had done then, realize the hopelessness of it all, and be willing to accept the pittance Frank Sutter would offer them. They could go away after that, forget the Ute Valley, the Lazy J, Sagebrush Hills, Skull Flats—all of it—find a place where there were no Frank Sutters.

The big worry was in the meantime—the need to keep matters going along on an even, if monotonous basis until Clint accepted the fate that had been dealt them. For herself, April was willing to take Sutter's offer at that very instant, pack up their belongings and turn her back on the home that had once meant so much to her.

Clint would not hear of it, and the one time she had suggested it, he had flown into a rage, accused her of knuckling under to Frank Sutter— of being afraid of him . . . She guessed she was, in a way. Actually she didn't give it much thought; she was interested only in keeping Clint alive until he could grow up and face the bitter facts of life.

And Sutter?

He was in no hurry. He knew he had but to stand by, wait. The Jackman place was slowly but surely falling apart, day by day, and with each crumbling adobe block, each splintering, rotting board, the property became less valuable on a dollar and cents basis. When the time came that the Jackmans had nothing left—no cattle, no money, no way to turn, odds were good he'd be able to get the place for back taxes and a couple a hundred dollars.

April came to the end of the planted row, paused to draw a breath, brush again at the sweat that persisted on collecting along her nose. It was hotter that day than the one before—or so it seemed. All days were hot, she guessed, she just noticed them now that she was forced to work more in the open.

Her thoughts came to a halt. A jab of fear, of surprise, rocked her. A man was standing beside a clump of doveweed—not ten feet away. He was a big man, wore a faded red shirt, patched gray pants that were badly torn; run-down boots, sweat-stained hat and, oddly, tight-fitting leather gloves. He was not armed.

His face was covered with several days' growth of dark whiskers and his eyes, a colorless gray in their deep caverns, had a haunted, lost quality to them.

"Who—" April began, wishing she had not left the rifle she sometimes brought with her, back at the house, "are you? What do you—"

"Lady," the man's long lips, cracked and dry, parted slightly, "I'd be obliged to you for a drink of water."

Without waiting for her to reply, he staggered on, trampling one of the tomato plants in his eagerness to cross the yard and reach the watering trough.

# CHAPTER TWO

There was a time when Clint Jackman had looked forward to driving into Cabezo for supplies. But that was before his pa had been felled by a bushwhacker's bullet. It had been different then; the Jackman name drew respect, stood for a fine ranch, a good herd—and money.

Now all that had changed. There was no one left in the valley to challenge Frank Sutter and, accordingly, the folks who worked and lived in town, cowpunchers, peddlers—all kowtowed to Frank Sutter and jumped like pricked frogs to do his bidding.

He'd never kowtow to any man, Clint told himself fiercely, no matter what. Sutter could even order his men to beat him, and he'd not crawl. They could hooraw him, plague him, play their smart-alec tricks on him, and he'd not give in; he'd never give them the satisfaction of seeing him knuckle under. He was a Jackman and someday, yes sir, someday, he'd make that name again mean something in the Ute River country.

If only he could get things started! That was the big catch. Right now he and April seemed to be hung up in a sort of snare—one in which they could neither stand still nor run. The squeeze was on them good, put there by Frank Sutter who was just holding off, waiting patiently, like one of the buzzards that flapped around Skull Flats, ready to take over when they reached the point where they could no longer keep going . . . He had to hold off that day—somehow. The ranch meant too much to April—and to him . . . He just had to figure out some way.

Clint slapped at the old mare with the reins in a sudden burst of determination. He'd just plain never let that happen! Somehow he'd get things going again—start the ranch on the road to recovery—and prosperity. He could just see himself then, riding right up to Sutter, and maybe Monte Fox and some of the others who worked for him, laughing in their faces. They'd eat crow—and plenty of it.

Problem was, how to get things started. Their first need was for cattle—and it took cash money to buy stock. The bank had turned them down flat when he'd gone there with April to see about a loan. Frank Sutter was probably behind that. Anyway, the banker had said no and there wasn't any other place to turn to.

The herd, except for about three hundred head, had all been sold off just before his pa had been murdered—and it had been the money for it the bushwhacker had gotten away with. Thus he and April had sure been left in a tight—one that, try as they both did, they seemed unable to work out of.

Glum, he stared over the mare's bobbing head at the scrubby growth covering Skull Flats as the buckboard rattled steadily along through the morning heat. They were little better than beggars—he and April—when you got right down to it; they were living on credit extended by John Larkin, credit guaranteed incidentally by twenty steers that had to be surrendered next spring in time for the general drive to Wichita.

They'd be square with old Larkin again then—there might even be a few dollars left over, it all depending on the price steers would be bringing at the time; but that really wouldn't mean much. The whole thing would just start all over again. Twenty more beeves would have to be pledged to Larkin to cover their needs in the months that followed; and the herd would be that much smaller.

It didn't sound like much—twenty steers—but when you didn't have many to start with and there wasn't much of a calf drop, and the rustlers just kept helping themselves, it sort of made for a losing battle. He'd have to admit that but he guessed he'd better not say it in front of April.

Cabezo, no more than two dozen buildings and houses, was just ahead. Larkin's General Store, Garcia's Livery Stable, the Alhambra Saloon, Heyman's Feed Company, Doc Haley's office, Gordon's Gun & Harness Shop, the Ute Hotel, the marshal's jail—he knew each by heart,

every cracked glass, split board, warped door—
and dreaded them all for now they reflected,
somehow, his inability to do anything about the
lives of his sister and himself, and the destiny of
the once proud Lazy J.

The street was empty but there were horses
standing at the hitchrack of the Alhambra . . .
Sutter horses, he noted with a sinking feeling.
Likely they were being ridden by Monte Fox
and Charlie Heer; seemed those two were always
hanging around the saloon. Didn't they ever have
to work like other punchers? Maybe they were
being paid special by Frank Sutter to just lay
around, do only certain jobs.

He guided the mare down the street, swung
into Larkin's wagonyard, which was across the
street from the store itself, and pulled to a halt.
Climbing down he tied the horse to the bar,
absently noting the minister's wife puttering
around in the flower garden next to the church,
hearing clearly, the clean, sharp ring of the
anvil coming from the blacksmith's shop. A
lean mongrel appeared at the side of Gordon's,
eyed him furtively, and then ducked into the
passageway separating that structure from its
neighbor. Somewhere a child was crying fret-
fully. . . .

These were good, friendly sights and sounds,
but they no longer stirred Clint Jackman as once
they had. Now, like the town's street, they were

irritants, factors in a denial and he found no pleasure in them.

Stepping away from the wagon, he moved through the deserted lot, crossed the street and climbed up onto Larkin's wide porch. The merchant was leaning against a counter at the rear of the crowded room as he entered.

Larkin, a small, rotund man with dark, expressionless eyes, nodded, neither cordial nor hostile, but simply neutral, and waited while Clint dug into his pocket for the list April had written out. Taking it in his fingers, Larkin glanced over it, pursed his thin lips.

"Quite a few items here, boy."

"Only what we need," Clint replied stiffly. They went through the same routine every time; the merchant doubtful, protesting, Clint assuring him—and each time an inner fury shook the boy into a helpless sort of frustration. "Deal we've got with you don't allow for any trimmings."

Larkin wagged his head. "At this rate you're liable to run over your credit limit."

Clint's anger surfaced. "We do, why, I reckon we can scare up an extra steer or two to satisfy you!"

The merchant shrugged. "Suppose so—leastwise I hope so. Don't like waiting a whole year for my money—think you ought to know that."

"Maybe you'd rather we'd do our trading

somewheres else!" Clint flared, a streak of the old Jackman independence asserting itself.

John Larkin smiled. "Now, just where would you go? Seventy miles to Vegas—and I misdoubt you'd find a storekeeper there willing to carry you on these terms—and under present circumstances."

"Present circumstances," Clint repeated, frowning. "That mean Frank Sutter?"

The merchant glanced closely at the boy, said, "I'd be a mite careful about that lip, was I you." Then putting his attention to the list again, added, "Some of these things I'll have to trim . . . Short on stock—"

"I want what's on there—just the way it's put down," Clint said stubbornly. "April knows what we've got to have. She ain't buying nothing we can do without."

"All right, all right," Larkin murmured, lifting a hand to calm the boy. "Only thinking of you— and the fact that one of these days you'll be running out of cattle and—"

"Aim to have something worked out long before then," Clint said in a firm voice, and turned toward the front of the store. "Got plans . . . How long it take to get that order ready?"

"Half hour, more or less. You got something to do, go ahead."

Clint halted behind the dust-filmed window fronting the street. He wished he was old enough to walk over to the Alhambra, go in and have himself a cold beer like he'd seen other punchers do, but he knew Tom Case, who owned the saloon, wouldn't serve him. Besides, that bunch from Sutter's was there, and he'd as soon avoid them this time, if he could. Last trip in they'd given him a pretty bad rousting around.

Idly he began to move about the store, wandering among the piles of kitchenware and ranch needs on display. They needed a couple of new water buckets—and that old washtub April was using leaked like a sieve—but they'd have to make do. Just as soon as he got things started though, he'd come in . . .

He shrugged off the often-voiced promise to himself, turned back to the window. Doc Haley was crossing over from his combination residence and office, headed for the hotel. He was carrying his black bag. Somebody over there sick, Clint guessed.

Abruptly he drew to attention. Four men were pushing through the Alhambra's batwings . . . Fox and Heer, as he had suspected, along with two other of Sutter's crew—Linus Kirby and Dave Bruner, who was a sort of gunslinger.

Clint watched them halt on the saloon's gallery, rake the street in their insolent king-of-the-mountain manner, come to a pause as their eyes settled on the mare and the buckboard in Larkin's wagonyard. Monte Fox said something.

All laughed, and then in a loose, shambling group, they sauntered toward the store.

Clint felt his muscles tighten, his nerves begin to prickle. He was in for it again. Might as well get set, but if only once—just once he could hold his own with them, laugh at them—tell them to go to hell!

"Hey, Larkin!" Monte Fox's grating voice reached in from the street. "You be real careful now and don't try cheating that there big rancher you're waiting on!"

The storekeeper glanced up, studied Clint for a moment, and then shaking his head, resumed his work.

"Tell him to come on out," Charlie Heer said, his voice also loud and irritating. "It ain't often us poor cowpokes gets a look at a big rancher. You know what—I hear tell him and his sister are running that big ranch all by themselves! Now, ain't that something?"

Clint, face burning, looked to the storekeeper, gathering up the items of the order he'd stacked on the counter. He was putting them in a small wooden box.

"Mister Jackman, you hear us? We'd sure be obliged was you to come out."

Clint cut back through the store, waited at the counter while the merchant tucked the last of the articles in the carton, and then, tight-lipped, hoisted it to his shoulder.

"Maybe—if you'd use the back door—"

Clint shook his head at the merchant's suggestion, started for the porch. Since the wagon was across the street, he'd be forced to pass by them, regardless; anyway he wasn't going to run.

"Here comes the big ranch man now," Fox yelled, grinning broadly. Grasping the handle of the screen door, he pulled it open, bowed deeply. Charlie Heer, Bruner, and the lanky Kirby were squatting on their heels in the street, just off the porch.

"You reckon we ought to help him with that there box he's a-carrying?" Monte continued, stepping up close to Clint.

"You leave me alone!" the boy said, jerking away and hurrying across the gallery.

John Larkin appeared in the doorway of his store, seemed about to say something. Monte Fox threw a hard glance at him and the merchant turned away without speaking.

"We don't aim to hurt you, Mister Jackman," Charlie Heer said. "Only aiming to help." Reaching up he tried to pull the box of grocery items from Clint's hands. The boy held tight, moved on.

He gained the street, started across. Bruner lazily thrust out a hand, caught the boy by the ankle. Clint tripped, almost fell.

Bruner said, "That there sister of your'n, she still the looker she used to be? You tell her I'd be mighty happy to drop by, do some of her chores for her if—"

"You shut up about my sister!" Clint yelled, whirling. "You hear? Don't you never say nothing from your filthy mouth about her again!"

He had halted in the center of the street, a wild fury gripping him so tightly that he trembled. Dave Bruner cocked his head to one side, studied Clint slyly.

"Now, just what would you do was I to come calling out there some night, boy? You think you're big enough to keep me out of the house?"

Frustration ripped through Clint. He stared at the grinning face, shouted: "Maybe I ain't, but I'm getting somebody who is! You'll see—you'll sure see!"

Monte Fox's liquor-flushed face sobered. His mouth became a thin line. "You're doing what?"

"Getting us somebody to help!" Clint blurted. "A gunman, that's what. You won't be pushing him around!"

Charlie Heer laughed, slapped at his leg. "Them—a-hiring themselves a gunslick! Why, they're too poor to be buying bullets for him!"

Clint swallowed hard, wished he could get to the buckboard. But he'd brought the four men up short, given them something to think about—and, anyway, it was too late now; the lie was out. Might as well go whole-hog; there was no difference in being hung for a sheep any more than for a goat.

"Not hiring one," he said loudly. "Man's a friend. Old friend of Pa's, in fact."

Bruner's features were still. "He got a name?"

Clint managed a thin smile. "Never you mind about that. You'll be hearing soon enough . . . Maybe even too soon."

Dave Bruner shrugged, hitched at the pistol slung at his side. "Sounds like a lot of bullshit to me. Ain't nobody coming in here, taking up for a ragtag, run down outfit like they got."

"You'll see," Clint said, continuing on toward the buckboard. "Just you wait."

The four riders watched him in silence. John Larkin was again standing in his doorway, and others on down the street, attracted by the shouting and laughing, had heard Clint's declaration as well.

The boy reached the vehicle, stowed the box in the bed and jerked the tie rope free. Throwing a covert look at Fox and the others, now eying him thoughtfully from Larkin's porch, he climbed onto the seat and took up the reins.

A glorious sort of exhilaration was rushing through him. He'd got the best of Monte and the others! For the first time he'd come out on top! Cutting the buckboard about, he headed into the street. On sudden impulse, he veered nearer the building, and spurred by heady victory, favored the punchers with a crooked smile.

"Don't any of you go leaving the country," he said, and touched the mare with the whip.

# CHAPTER THREE

April followed the stranger to the trough, circling somewhat to maintain a respectable distance. There was no fear, as such, in her, only a caution. In silence, she watched him duck his head into the water, raise it, leaving the wealth of near black hair plastered to his skull, while rivulets streamed off onto his shoulders and down his neck.

Cupping his gloved hands, he filled his mouth, held the water there, not swallowing but allowing it to trickle down his throat slowly. He repeated the process several times, and then lowering his head again, drank greedily. After that he came about. Leaning against the heavy plank trough, he faced the girl.

"Wasn't aiming to frighten you," he said in an apologetic voice.

April shook her head. "You didn't. Surprised, mostly. Never expected anyone to come walking in from that direction. Lose your horse?"

He nodded. "Yesterday morning. Bluff give way under him, broke his neck." He reached down, scooped up another handful of water, rubbed it across his lips as if endeavoring to force moisture into the parched tissues.

31

April was staring at him. "You walked across the Sagebrush Hills?"

"Hills," he muttered in an almost angry tone. "I've crossed mountains that weren't as mean as your hills."

"I know," she said. "It's terrible country. I'm surprised that you made it—with no water or food—and on foot."

He shrugged, again brushed at his mouth. "There a town close?"

"Cabezo, but it's not very close. A half a day's ride . . . You could have gone in with my brother if you'd got here earlier." April stopped, realizing how the statement must have sounded to him. It was like saying he should have arrived sooner—crossed the Sagebrush Hills and gotten there on time—if he wanted a ride. "You must be hungry," she said lamely, in an effort to cover up.

"Some," he admitted. "Ate yesterday morning, however, so I'm not too bad off. Was the water I needed."

He drew himself up straight. There were ragged holes in the knees of worn pants, April noticed, and a few cactus needles were sticking in the leather of his left-hand glove. Evidently he'd fallen several times during his passage across the hills.

"You sure you're not hurt, Mr.—Mr.—"

"Matt Rusk. I'm all right. Maybe a bit wore

32

down, but that don't amount to anything. Been that way before . . . What should I call you?"

She liked the way he spoke, quiet, somewhat slow, but direct. She said: "I'm April Jackman. My brother Clint and I own this ranch."

He nodded, allowed his eyes to stray around the yard, take in the sad, neglected look of it all. He was making his estimation, having his wonderment, she knew, but he'd make no comment on it.

"Clint will be back from town shortly," she said, realizing they were still standing there in the open. "I was about to fix dinner. If you can hold out for a little longer, you can eat with us . . . Then we'll see about getting you in to town."

"Obliged," he said quietly, and lowered his head.

April looked at him narrowly. There was something in his tone, his manner, that said he was one who accepted any and all things that came to him—good or bad—with indifferent resignation. He was a man uncaring, not for himself, not for anyone—not for anything; one who was alive, who lived and nothing more. She wondered at the cause, and turning, started toward the house.

"It'll be cooler on the porch," she said.

Wordless, he trailed after her, his height making her own taller-than-average frame for a woman, seem small. They reached the house and she pointed to a rocking chair on the gallery that her father had favored.

"Sit there. I'll find you something to nibble on until dinner's ready."

Rusk nodded, sank into the rocker. April entered her kitchen, returned presently with a cup of black coffee and a wedge of dried apricot pie.

"Coffee's not hot," she said, "but maybe it'll help a little."

"Be fine," he murmured, half rising at her approach, and then settled back. He drank the coffee before she had even reached the door on her return. When she glanced over her shoulder he was eating the pie, savoring each bite with obvious relish.

Clint Jackman was in no hurry to reach the ranch. With each passing mile the enormousness of the lie—actually the threat—he had blurted while in the grip of outraged anger, became more apparent to him.

How could he make good on such a statement? There was no way. He sighed deeply, unseeing eyes on the rump of the patient old mare plodding steadily along on the familiar road to home . . . One thing sure, he just couldn't go back to town again—at least, not for a long spell. He couldn't face all those people there—not only Monte Fox and the other punchers from Sutter's, but the folks who'd been standing around listening—and who'd lost no time telling everybody else that hadn't been handy.

April had suggested several times that she ought to make the trip in for supplies. He had always refused, knowing she was making the offer simply to prevent his being humiliated at the hands of the Sutter crowd . . . He guessed now he'd have to agree to such an arrangement.

But that was the least serious of his worries, he realized with a sudden start. Fox and the others appeared to believe him when he told them that a man—a gunman—was coming to help out at the ranch. They'd repeat that bit of information to Frank Sutter, and Sutter, in order to protect what he considered his future interests, might make some sort of immediate move to take over the ranch he'd long coveted.

If so, he and April were in for a bad time, Clint thought, and moaned softly. Why hadn't he kept his big mouth shut? Why did he have to blow up, say the things he had? If only he could have kept his head, not let them rile him like they always did . . . He guessed it was that Dave Bruner talking about April that set him off—but there was no use thinking about it now. It was done and there was no taking words back once you've said them . . . Thing to worry about was what to do next.

He could solve the part pertaining to his pride by letting April have her way, make the trip into

Larkin's the next time they needed supplies . . . No! His thoughts rebelled at that solution and a trickle of shame moved through him. He was thinking like a little kid; he'd stirred up the problem, he'd accept the consequences. He'd be a coward to run away from it.

Maybe it wouldn't be so bad after all—as bad as he figured, anyway. He'd just go right on into town as usual, and keep his jaws clamped shut. If anything was said, he'd just give whoever said it a cold eye, sort of pass the idea along that the man they were looking for hadn't arrived yet. Might be the whole mess would work out better for him; could be, henceforth, he'd be treated with a little respect . . .

Frank Sutter . . .

His mind came to grips with that problem again, settled on dead center. He'd best be trying to come up with some kind of an answer for the repercussions that were bound to come from that quarter, and stop worrying about his pride.

They couldn't just up and fight Sutter. That would be crazy—and the quickest way to die he could think of. Not that Sutter wouldn't welcome the chance to settle things with a gun—as long as it looked all right to others, and that he, being the injured party, had had no choice but to resort to guns—and that's the way Frank Sutter would make it appear.

He might send down ten gunhands, all experts,

to take over from just him and April, but the way it would turn out, folks would believe that he and April had made the first move, had actually attacked the gunhands, and they'd been forced to shoot in order to protect themselves. Sutter had that kind of a cold-blooded mind, and that kind of power in the valley; he could make people swallow any yarn he liked.

How was he going to explain all this to April?

Clint brushed nervously at the sweat on his forehead. Oh, he guessed she would understand all right; April was that way—but the shame, the guilty feeling he had from plunging them deeper into an already bad situation was hard to bear.

Maybe the answer was to hire a man. Maybe that was the thing to do—bargain away another twenty steers, or thirty if that's what it took, and with the cash received pay a gunslinger to come to the ranch, hang around, look after their interests.

But such would only postpone the end. They couldn't keep a man there forever, and unless he could come up with that idea on how to get the ranch going again, there'd be no real purpose in it anyway; it was just a question of time until Frank Sutter would close in, take over—the duration of that time having direct relation to the number of steers in their steadily decreasing herd. When the last one was gone—they were finished.

Clint sighed, wiped at his eyes. It was a hopeless situation, made even more so by his thoughtless actions. He could forget about a gunman; they didn't have the money to pay one—it wasn't practical—and he hadn't the slightest idea how you went about hiring one even if they were able to do so. Best thing was to make a clean breast of the whole mess to April, let her decide what was best to do. Maybe it was just as well they give up now, let Sutter have his way . . . That would settle matters for good.

He raised his eyes. The gate to the ranch was just ahead, its familiar, bleached posts showing cracks where the elements were taking their toll. The house was looking old, too, he noticed. The roof over the front gallery sagged at one end, and the floor had a slight tilt to it. Other things showed signs of age and wear, too, and he should do something about repairing and replacing— but somehow it seemed there was never time . . . Keeping an eye on the herd, doing all the things that just had to be done, didn't leave any time for extras.

A smile pulled at his lips as he sniffed the air. April was baking light bread. The good smell of it reached him, brushed away briefly all the worries that beset his young mind . . . Dinner would be about ready. He'd eat, then he'd sit down with April, tell her everything that had happened in town.

He rounded the corner of the house, entered the yard. A frown pulled at his brow as an unfamiliar figure on the porch, occupying his pa's rocking chair, caught his attention. He leaned forward, looking more closely . . . A big, hard-faced man with cold, lifeless eyes—a stranger.

# CHAPTER FOUR

Matt Rusk stirred as the buckboard rolled into the yard. This would be April Jackman's brother returning from town. He remained motionless, watched the boy pull up to one of the canted hitchracks and halt, drop to the ground and take a box of groceries from the bed of the vehicle.

Rusk was surprised to note the youth of the boy; fourteen, perhaps fifteen—certainly no more than that. He wasn't large, either, ran somewhat to gawkiness, but he had the same dark hair and fine, large eyes as his sister. That something troubled him was apparent; the ranch itself, Matt supposed; it was decaying, falling apart around their ears, and the boy was too young, too inexperienced to stop the disintegration. The two seemed to be the only ones on the place; he wondered about that. Where was everyone else? There surely were others around.

He heard a sound at the kitchen door, pulled himself to his feet as April stepped into the open, wiping her hands on a red checked apron. He hadn't paid too much attention to her at first meeting, not being in an exactly appreciative frame of mind, but now, after a quenched thirst, a piece of delicious pie and a cup of coffee, he was aware of the nicer things in life . . . April Jackman was a most attractive woman, he saw.

She greeted Clint as he came up onto the porch, halted him. Nodding to Matt, she said: "This is Mr. Rusk . . . My brother, Clint, Mr. Rusk."

It was impersonal, polite introduction, served notice to both that Matt Rusk was just a passerby, a dinner guest—and nothing more.

Clint, his brow wrinkled, nodded to Matt, said, "Howdy," and managed to balance the box long enough to extend a hand. There was a suppressed glow in his eyes, however, a sly, quiet consideration that was weighing and taking account of possibilities.

"Glad to know you," Rusk said. "Your sister's been kind enough to invite me for a meal."

Clint's attention was on Matt's hands, on the snug leather gloves that encased them. "Good . . . Good," he mumbled. "Always fine—having company."

"Put the box in the pantry," April said, breaking a somewhat awkward pause. "We can eat as soon as you're ready."

Clint moved on by, his features serious. The girl watched him for a moment, a puzzled look in her eyes, indicating that she, too, had taken note of the boy's disturbed manner. She made no comment, however, and turned to Matt.

"I hope you didn't mind waiting—"

"Not at all. Regular meals are something I'm

sort of a stranger to," he replied, and followed her into the kitchen.

The room was hot from the big, nickel-trimmed cook stove in one corner, and April crossed to a door in the opposite wall, opened it, allowed a draft to sweep through and bring some relief. Clint was already at the table. Rusk paused behind his chair, waited for April to be seated.

"Smelled that light bread clean back to the Flats—almost," the boy said, spreading butter on a thick chunk.

Rusk nodded. "Nothing quite smacks of home like fresh, hot bread," he said in a low, wistful voice.

April passed the platter of fried meat and potatoes to him, noting that he had not removed the gloves. She wondered, absently, if he ever took them off.

"Where is home?"

He was careful, almost slow in his movements, forking out a piece of the steak, raking off a quantity of the golden brown potato slices.

"Montana, I suppose . . . Worked a lot of places."

Clint was leaning forward, elbows on the table fascinated by the gloves, by the powerful slope of Rusk's thick shoulders, by the tough, hard-bitten cut of his features.

"You have to leave there—Montana, I mean—for some reason?" he asked blandly.

Rusk did not look up from his plate. "Man usually moves for one reason or another."

The boy's tone was hopeful. "The law—was that the rea—"

"Clint!" April broke in, shocked and angry.

Matt Rusk smiled. "No, law's not tracking me." Taking a second slice of bread, he dabbed it with butter. "Plenty of things can set a man to moving besides the law."

"Mr. Rusk came in from the Sagebrush Hills," April said, torn between a desire to hear more but not wanting to, either. "Lost his horse—walked in all the way from the buttes."

Clint whistled softly and his eyes spread. "How long it take you?"

"Since yesterday morning," April supplied before Matt could answer.

Again the boy whistled. "Can't do much better'n that on a horse."

"Rough country," Rusk admitted laconically, and continued with his meal.

He ate with the appreciation of a hungry man, one long without a plate of good food, yet going at it slowly, methodically, as if reluctant to finish, bring it all to an end.

"Mr. Rusk needs a ride into town," April said, passing the platter again to Matt. "I thought you'd like to drive him in."

Clint's face paled slightly, and then he smiled. "Sure. Be real glad to." He shifted his gaze to

Matt. "There somebody you're aiming to see?"

"Stranger here," Rusk said. "Looking for a job so's I can buy myself a horse and tack. Was headed for Texas and a job when I lost my sorrel."

"You a cowhand?"

"About all I know—cows."

The boy's face was a dark study. "You leave everything back there at the buttes with your horse—gun and all?"

"Everything. None of it was worth much. Pretty badly beat up."

"But a gun—man just don't go walking off across the hills without a gun—"

"Never carry one," Matt Rusk said in a gentle but firm voice that declared the matter closed.

Clint lowered his head, toyed with the food on his plate with a fork. In the silence that hung in the heat-filled room, April said: "More coffee, Mr. Rusk?"

"Thank you," he murmured, pushing forward his cup. "Take it as a favor if you'd call me Matt. Not used to being mister."

The girl smiled. "All right, Matt. And I'm April. My brother is Clint."

The boy nodded. "Sounds lots better. Was like being in church or something . . . Now it's like we were all friends." There was an eagerness to him. "Matt—"

Rusk paused, glanced at the boy. "Yeh?"

"Was just thinking, you need a job so's you can get yourself a horse and gear . . . We need somebody to help us around here—"

"Clint—" April broke in for the second time, her face showing concern.

Rusk touched her with a side look, saw the alarm, or perhaps recognized fear in her eyes, shook his head. Whatever it was, she disapproved.

"Wouldn't work out, I'm afraid. Be me getting the best of the deal."

"No you wouldn't! Come out about even-steven for all of us!"

April's lips were pressed tight. "I don't see what kind of work we'd have for Mr. Rusk to do . . . There's hardly anything left—"

"Why, there's plenty needs doing, April, and you know it! A lot of things need fixing—things that ought to get done but can't because I have to watch out for the herd and do the regular chores."

April was eying the boy closely. She knew him well, had been aware instantly from the look of him when he returned from town that something had happened; and now, with that instinctive insight peculiar to women where someone close to them is involved, she was wondering if that was the reason he wanted Matt Rusk to stay around the ranch for a while.

She could be wrong, she decided. It could

be that there being only the two of them on the place, Clint simply craved the company of another man—and Matt Rusk in his quiet, withdrawn manner, had captured his fancy . . . There could be a risk involved, too; Clint could get wrong ideas from Matt Rusk—not the outlaw sort of ideas, he didn't appear to be the outlaw type, but . . .

"What about it, April?"

"Maybe Matt doesn't want to stay," she replied, her manner softening. "He could have other plans, you know. Did say he was on his way to Texas."

"You got a job waiting for you there, Matt?" Clint asked in a rush of words.

Rusk's shoulders stirred. "No. Aimed to find one."

"Then there's no reason why you can't stay on here. We'll give you your pick of the horses we've got left . . . One thing we've sure got is horses. Running loose all over the place."

Matt slid another glance at the girl, shook his head. "Not so fast, boy. We've got no deal yet. Did intend to pay for my meal and a ride into town with some chores you'd figure up, but staying on long enough to pay for a horse and gear—"

"A month, it'd take—"

"Staying on a month, well, that's something that's up to your sister."

Clint swung eagerly to April. "It's all right with you, isn't it?"

The girl stared into her cup of coffee, now gone cold. It would be nice having a man—a grown man, around the place for a while. And it seemed to count a lot with Clint, for some mysterious reason . . . Things would be bad for him soon enough as it was; she should give in on this, let him have what she could give him now.

"I guess there are a few things that need doing—if Matt doesn't mind yard work."

"Work's work," Rusk said.

"Then it's settled!" Clint cried happily, and impulsively extended his hand across the table to Rusk. "Let's shake on it!"

Matt took the boy's fingers into his gloved hand gravely. "You're the boss, beginning now."

"Fine—fine! I'll show you around, tell you what—"

"Not now," April broke in firmly. "Matt's in no condition to go traipsing over the place today. Expect what he'd like is rest—sleep."

Clint's face fell. "I forgot," he said. "Just wasn't thinking, and I'm sorry."

"No need," Rusk said smilingly. "Am admitting to being a mite tired. That walk across your Sagebrush Hills was more than enough to take a man's wind."

"Tomorrow morning will be soon enough for

you to start work," April said rising. "Now, Clint, suppose you take Matt down to the bunkhouse, show him where he can sleep."

Clint, disappointment still registering in his eyes, nodded, got to his feet. Matt followed, glanced to the girl. "Something I can use—sleep. Expect I'll roll right around the clock."

April paused. "You mean you won't want any supper?"

"After a meal like that, I won't have any trouble waiting for breakfast. Sure am obliged to you."

"You're welcome, of course—and you don't need to thank me for your meal since you'll be working for it."

Rusk stepped back, moved toward the door. "Thanking you just the same. Cooking like you do is a sort of art, one any man ought to appreciate—and I'm one who does. Now, Clint, if you'll show me that bed, I'll crawl right into it."

The boy crossed the porch hastily, led the way to the bunkhouse and opened the partly unhinged door.

"Looks like a job for me right there," Matt said, eying the loose nails in the metal straps as he entered. Looking around the empty room, he said: "Reckon my choice is wide open, far as a bunk's concerned."

"Pick any you want," Clint replied, lounging against a wall. "Used to be more'n a dozen men sleeping here when my pa was alive and the ranch was going good."

Matt made no comment and Clint watched him move to the bed nearest the door and opposite the window; he would be choosing it since it was where the air was best.

"Matt—"

Rusk, in the process of gathering up the blankets from the bunk, and giving them a good shake outside to displace the accumulated dust, turned expectantly.

"Yeh?"

"I've got Pa's gun and holster outfit up at the house. I'll bring it down to you so's you can wear it."

Rusk walked to the door, snapped the bed covers vigorously, returned and began to spread them over the shuck mattress.

"Don't bother," he said. "Never carry one."

"But if you're going to be working around here on the ranch—"

Rusk's features were slack, expressionless. "There a need to go armed?"

"Well, no, I reckon there ain't no real need. Only it seems a man ought—" Clint's voice broke off. A frown cut deep into his forehead. He was quiet for a long minute, and then said: "You're not wanting to pack a gun—it have something to do with your hands—wearing those gloves like you do—I mean?"

Rusk wheeled slowly. His shoulders were forward, his craggy face stilled, and his gray eyes fathomless in their deep-set, shadowy pockets. There was an overall bleakness to him that even Clint, young as he was, could sense.

"Good night, boy," the older man said in a low voice, and turned to his bed.

# CHAPTER FIVE

Well before sunrise Matt Rusk came awake. He stood up abruptly in the center of the hushed bunkhouse, seemingly startled at discovering himself in such surroundings, and then grimacing self-consciously, crossed to the door. He felt good, completely rested and recovered from the ordeal across the Sagebrush Hills—a tribute to the animal vitality of the man.

Stepping out into the yard, he stood for a moment staring into the east where the pale flare of false dawn was pearling the sky. Someone was already up inside the house, he noted, seeing a faint curl of smoke beginning to twist upward from the chimney . . . April most likely, and at the thought of her he rubbed at the stubble on his cheeks. He needed a shave—and his razor was back with his other possessions on the dead sorrel. He'd borrow from the Jackmans. If Clint wanted to lend him something, let it be shaving gear.

He started for the horse trough, paused. There should be a place around behind the bunkhouse where the crew did their scrubbing up. He circled the building, spotted a lever pump and a bench under a small tree. Several rusting tin washpans lay on the ground nearby.

Choosing the best of the containers, he put it in proper line on the bench and tried the pump. The leathers had apparently dried from disuse, and the plunger simply moved up and down, creating no suction. Rusk considered the pump for a few moments. Perhaps it was not entirely out of service; it could just need priming. If that failed, he'd have to take the thing apart.

Grabbing the pan, he crossed to the trough, filled the container and returned to the pump. Working the lever with one hand, he poured the water slowly into the plunger slot in the top of the casting. Shortly the leather washers softened, caught, began to drag against the pump's throat. And then, reluctantly at first, water began to trickle from the spout.

Matt set the pan aside, continued to work the handle until he had a fair-sized stream of water belching from the pump with each down stroke. He grunted his satisfaction. With luck and regular use, the plunger should continue to produce without him having to go into repairs. Sliding the washpan under the spout, he filled it, started to remove his gloves and do a thorough job of cleaning up. A small sound brought him around.

It was April. In one hand she carried a bucket half-filled with steaming water; in the other were razor, soap, and mug. A leather strop hung across her forearm, while over her shoulder were draped several soft towels.

"Thought maybe you could use these things," she said. "They were my father's."

"Was planning to do some borrowing," he replied with a smile, and reached out.

She passed over the articles, unconsciously noting his gloved hands again. "Just keep it all here," she said, forcing herself to look away. "I—I see you got the pump to working."

"Was only dry," he said, laying out the equipment on the bench. He picked up the razor, examined it admiringly. "Fine bit of steel. I'll take good care of it."

April smiled, said: "Breakfast'll be ready by the time you are," and turned back for the house.

Using the water in the bucket, Matt lathered his face, and with a small piece of mirror someone had left wedged in a fork of the tree, proceeded to scrape off the whiskers he'd built up in the past few days.

The razor was somewhat dull and he was compelled to strop it several times before he succeeded in acquiring a comfortable edge. Like just about everything else around the place, he realized, it was going to hell for lack of use. Again he wondered what the story of the Jackman ranch might be. Once it had been a prosperous spread—it was easy to see that . . . Something had happened—something bad; now everything was wasting away—going to seed.

He finished his cleaning up, wished he had a better, or even just a change of clothing, but he didn't, and so dismissed it from his mind. He'd wash the shirt and socks that night, and first chance he got to go into town, he'd put out a dollar of his dwindling pocket capital for a new pair of pants. Falling as often as he had during that hike across the Sagebrush Hills had just about finished the ones he was wearing. From the knees down they were little better than shredded rags.

Gathering his toilet articles, he took them into the bunkhouse and placed them on a small table built into the wall. He noticed then the fair-sized, if wavy mirror above it, took a minute to better examine himself. He'd done a passable job with the chip wedged in the tree, guessed he looked almost human again.

Grinning humorlessly at the thought, and returning to the yard, he made his way to the main house. Clint was waiting at the door, ushered him into the room where April was piling crisp, lean bacon strips onto a plate already graced by several fried eggs. Rusk shook his head in wonder and surprise as he inhaled the delicious aroma.

"We've got us a couple of dozen chickens," Clint said. "Long as you're working here you'll have plenty of fresh eggs to eat."

Matt smiled at April, both understanding the

meaning behind the statement, and sat down to the table.

"Soon's you're finished," the boy said, "I'll show you around. I'm already done."

Rusk ate as quickly as possible, conscious of Clint's mounting impatience, and then again thanking the girl, followed him into the yard.

"Reckon you'd like to pick out your horse first thing," he said, heading toward a corral at the lower end of the yard.

"No hurry . . ."

"Well, you'll be needing something to ride— and I was thinking maybe you'd be wanting to go to town."

Matt nodded. "Was thinking of blowing myself to a new pair of britches," he said as they drew up to the enclosure in which a half a dozen horses had gathered in one corner.

"If you don't see one there you'd like, we got a bunch more running loose on the range. Have to round them up, though."

Matt singled out a close-coupled gelding that looked promising. The animal had a deep chest, lean shoulders and withers, carried his head well.

"Chestnut there—he looks good."

The boy bobbed his head. "Guess he is, but he's kind of mean. Was a puncher here by the name of Gates who was always trying to ride him. He did but he never could do much with him."

Matt glanced around. "Saddles in the barn?"

Clint pointed to a small shed off the larger structure. "Harness and stuff's in there. Take what you want."

Rusk picked himself a somewhat worn but comfortable and well made hull, a braided bridle with good reins, along with a thick wool blanket and a rope. Returning to the corral, he slung all across the top bar except the rope, and climbed down into the yard.

Flushing the horses out of the corner, he swung his loop, neatly caught the chestnut, and brought him about. The gelding began to fight at once, drawing back, shaking his head angrily as he strove to rear. Rusk, speaking steadily in a low voice, closed in relentlessly, shortening the rope gradually until finally he had the chestnut snubbed to a post.

He got the gear on with no trouble, but the instant he swung aboard, the horse began to run. He made two quick circuits of the corral, started then to sunfishing and plowing up the loose soil, scattering the other animals into all directions.

Matt, fighting to stay in a saddle with stirrups he'd neglected to check for length, finally brought the horse under control, swerved him in to where Clint was watching from the top of the corral.

"You sure tamed him down quick!" the boy said, eyes bright with excitement. "I'll bet you've done a lot of bronc breaking."

"My share," Rusk answered, swinging down and tugging at the straps and buckles to correct the stirrups. Once or twice he thought the chestnut was going to send him sailing over the fence—and he would have deserved it. He should have taken time to look the saddle over good, see that it fit properly . . . But there'd be no trouble now. The horse had been broken once, was only letting off a little ginger.

He stepped back into the saddle, settled his feet in the stirrups, tried them on for size. They were just right and he nodded agreeably to himself. It was good having a horse under him again—and the chestnut was a good animal, too.

"You don't mind," he said then, looking at Clint, "I'll keep him in the barn with the horses you're working regularly. Hate using a rope on him every time I want to ride."

"Sure, help yourself," the boy said quickly. "You just do whatever you like . . . Want to take a ride over the ranch now?"

Matt rode the chestnut through the corral gate, dropped the wire loop back over the post, and started for the barn.

"If it's all the same to you, think I'll pass that up for a spell. Walked across a fair-sized chunk of it yesterday, and there's a few chores I ought to get out of the way before I do any sightseeing."

Clint's face reflected momentary disappointment, but cleared quickly. "Expect I ought to be having a look at the herd, anyway," he said. "If I don't keep a sharp watch, the rustlers'll have us picked clean . . . Ain't stole nothing now for over a week."

Matt only nodded, showing little interest in the problem. He reached the barn, left the saddle and led the chestnut into one of the empty stalls. He'd leave the gear on the horse for a time, get him accustomed to wearing leather again. Seeing to fresh hay and a quantity of grain in the manger, Rusk returned to the yard.

Clint was moving off, astride a small, wiry buckskin and riding bareback. Matt glanced around, undecided where to begin; almost everything, it seemed, cried for attention. April's supply of split wood for the kitchen stove was low. That appeared to be the most pressing chore. Pulling off his faded shirt, he headed for the chopping block.

# CHAPTER SIX

Rusk worked steadily, first splitting the dry logs, then cutting them to proper stove-box lengths which he tossed then into a growing mound. He'd not try to clean up the entire pile at once, he decided, rather would plug away at it a couple of hours each morning, until the sun became too hot, then turn to less vigorous tasks. Putting in time every day for a week or so with the ax should build a supply that would last April for quite a spell.

Sweat glistening on his back and shoulders, he paused to draw a long breath, rest briefly. He'd done about enough for one session, guessed he'd turn to something else . . . The screen door at the main house slammed. He brushed moisture from his eyes, glanced up. April, carrying a glass and a pitcher of cool water from the crock in the springhouse, was coming toward him. He grinned his pleasure, and burying the blade of the ax in a log, moved in under the shade of a nearby tree.

"You look like you could use a cold drink," the girl said, handing him the glass and filling it to the brim.

Matt nodded appreciatively. "Can work up a steam quick at this."

April looked at the woodpile, pursed her lips.

59

"You've cut a lot in a couple of hours. More there now than I usually had waiting when we had regular hired help."

Matt studied his glass. "That a long time ago?"

"A year now, almost—since we had any help."

He extended the container for a refill. He could understand now why everything appeared to be in such disrepair. Keeping up a place the size of the Jackmans' was a chore in itself without trying to raise cattle as well.

"Big job," he said. "Ever think of selling out?"

April's slender shoulders stirred. Turning, she placed the pitcher on the bench built against the trunk of the tree, and sat down. She looked fresh and cool in a light, cotton dress of blue and white . . . Her hair, he noted, was a deep brown with reddish high lights where the sun's direct rays touched it.

"It's the only home I—we—have ever known," she said. "Hard to give it up—and Clint has such hopes for getting it going again." She paused, a frown tugging at her dark brows as she looked off toward the southwest range. "He should be coming back."

Rusk handed her the glass. She set it beside the pitcher.

"Going to be tough, starting a ranch without cattle."

She nodded wearily, said, "Which we can't buy, even if we had the money."

"Why not?"

"Man by the name of Sutter. Frank Sutter. He's been after our place for years. Always wanted to buy it. After Pa was ambushed and robbed, he tried just about everything to make us give it up."

"You mean—more than just an offer to buy?"

"Lots more. There's been several raids—men wearing masks, shooting up the place. They killed our dog and a couple of horses one time. Our old milk cow was shot. Then we've had fires out on the range—and the rustling, of course . . . It never stops."

Rusk was pressing his gloved hands together, palms tight, chafing them as if they were cold. "You mean it's this Sutter who's stealing your cattle?"

"No, not him—he'd not bother with a little thing like that. He's the biggest rancher in the valley. If he had our place, he'd own everything east of the Sagebrush Hills to the Trail, and that would probably make his ranch the largest in the whole Territory, except maybe the Maxwell outfit . . . No, he's not taking our cattle, but he knows all about it."

"Rustling's every rancher's worry, no matter who's getting hurt. He and all the rest of the cattle growers around here ought to step in, put an end to it."

"They would—if Father was still alive. But they won't turn a hand now, knowing that Frank

Sutter wants it this way. He figures it will finally break us—and then he can take over."

Matt Rusk shifted. "World's full of Frank Sutters, it seems."

She looked at him curiously, wondering at the defeat in his tone. It was almost as if he were afraid of trouble—and that was hard to believe. He looked so strong, so undeniable—yet she sensed a type of withdrawal in him, a reluctance to face up to anything other than a normal, orderly procession of events.

"I suppose so," she murmured, "but they should be brought to task, not let run rough-shod over people and let have their way."

"Man with power can just about do as he pleases. Seems to be the rule."

"Perhaps, but it's still wrong and folks ought to stand up, do something about it." Her glance was again reaching beyond the yard. Small worry lines showed at the corners of her mouth.

"You want me to go look for him?" Rusk suggested.

Her lips tightened, but she shook her head. "Not yet . . . It would shame him—and he's trying so hard to be a man, carry a man's load."

Matt shrugged, looked at her keenly. "Answer's still to sell out to Sutter if you're afraid for Clint. Nothing's worth him getting hurt—and by quitting you'll avoid trouble."

Either his choice of words, or the fact that it

was pure truth, stirred a flame of anger within in April Jackman. "I take it that's your answer to everything—avoid trouble!"

The edge to her voice was lost on him. "Had my share, and then some. Not looking for more. Seems smart to me to back off when you're up against something you know you can't lick."

"Clint doesn't see it that way! Insists we can get the ranch working again, if we'll just hang on, keep trying—and I think he's right!"

She was unaccountably on the defense. Rusk merely shook his head. "Yet you're scared when he's out of your sight—on your own range—for more'n a couple of hours."

April flushed, trapped by the contradiction. "Not that . . . It's only I—"

"You don't owe me an explanation, but someday you'll have to make up your mind about him—what you want for him and what you intend to do where this Frank Sutter's concerned. It's a choice you won't be able to dodge."

"And if I can't make that choice?"

"Then just forget it—move on," he said flatly, harshly. "I've found few things in this life worth the price you're asked to pay."

"In so many words then, your answer to a problem—a serious one, is to forget it—run . . ."

He considered her in a patient sort of way, made no reply. A collared lizard, looking like some prehistoric monster in miniature, scrambled up onto the chopping block, viewed them critically with beady eyes. April shifted, smoothed the wrinkles in her lap.

"Well, I'm not built that way. Neither is Clint. We were taught, and believe in, fighting for what's ours."

Matt Rusk gave her a dry smile. "A good way to be—only is it worth getting hurt for—maybe even losing a life over?"

"Clint has to be a man!" she snapped, and then relief flooded her eyes as Clint, hunched low on the buckskin, broke through the brush at the far end of the yard.

He rode up to the cottonwood, slid from the horse and faced them, trembling with rage.

"Rustlers again!" he shouted. "Two more steers—one was that old brindle we've had around for a long time. Other'n was a yearling."

"Oh, Clint, are you sure?" April said in a falling voice.

"Of course I'm sure! We ain't got so many cows that I don't miss one or two when they're gone." The boy replied, taking up the glass and pitcher of water. His glance touched the pile of split wood, came back to Matt. "You've been working mighty hard, seems."

April waited until he had downed a glass of water. Then: "Did you see any sign of the rustlers?"

The boy shook his head. "Same bunch, know that. Tracks head west, then get lost in the rocks—just like they always do."

April plucked at the edge of her apron. "That's eight head this month . . . At this rate we can hardly—"

"Why don't you get the sheriff or the town marshal, whatever you've got around here, to take a hand," Rusk broke in. "His job to do something about it."

"Avery Kingstreet?" Clint said scornfully. "He won't do nothing. Sutter's told him not to—and they both know it's probably that Henderson bunch doing it."

"Henderson?"

"Squatters, down along the edge of the brakes."

"Anybody ever go there to see?"

"Sure," Clint said, casting a side glance at April. "Rode down there once. Didn't see any of our beef and when I asked old man Henderson, he just laughed at me.

"Way it was, he'd been sort of helping himself for years. Always did when Pa was alive. Pa knew about it, never did anything. Said the Henderson children had to eat . . . Felt sorry for them, I reckon . . . Trouble is now they've got the habit. Help themselves whenever they please to what they want—not just a steer every couple of months."

April Jackman's face was tight, angry. "Clint,

you're not to go there again—do you hear? I won't have you—"

"Henderson's stealing our cattle," the boy said stubbornly. "Leastwise, I'm pretty sure he is— and he's got to quit it . . . I'm just hoping one of these days I'll catch him and that Jesse at it, and I'll have me a rifle along! I'll make them stop."

"You're not to even try and stop them. If we ever actually see the Hendersons stealing, then we'll go to Avery Kingstreet, demand he do something."

Clint wagged his head. "He won't. Sutter's done told him not to, no matter what . . . Going to be up to me."

Matt Rusk turned away, reached for his shirt and began to pull it on. The lizard, frightened from his high perch by Clint's arrival and now crouched beside a log, took off in sudden, frantic flight, running high on his bent legs. Matt watched the reptile disappear into the weeds beyond the woodpile. Lizards were smarter than people; they knew when they were overmatched and accepted the alternative.

*Like me,* he thought, hooking the last button on his shirt. A man was a fool to buck the odds. There were times when you couldn't win regardless of what was right and what was wrong; nor did being right guarantee anything. Nothing was ever as clear cut as that.

And the Jackmans?

It was a sad situation, one in which they couldn't possibly come out on top under present conditions. This Sutter was evidently the big whip in the country and what he wanted, he got—one way or another. The girl and her brother would be smart to sell, take what they could get and move on before one, or both, of them got hurt . . . That was the solution whether they liked it or not.

He nodded to April and then to Clint. If they came to him for advice, that was what he'd tell them. He'd tried to get the point over to the girl, but he'd failed. Maybe she'd see the wisdom of it after she thought it over for a bit.

"Got some doors that need fixing," he said, and started for the bunkhouse. Halfway he heard the boy's voice, high pitched in outrage.

"I'm taking Pa's shotgun—lay out there in the brush and wait. I ain't standing for old Henderson or anybody else rustling any more of our cattle, April—and you ain't going to stop me!"

"You'll do nothing of the kind," the girl replied in a firm, steady way. "You think I want you shot down like Pa was? . . . We'll get along best we can. We're not broke yet, and maybe something will change—turn up . . ."

Matt Rusk closed his ears to the hope in April Jackman's voice. He fancied he could almost detect accusation in its essence. He swore silently. No—he'd not let himself in for anything.

He'd managed for five years to avoid strife—sometimes at the cost of being considered less than a man—why this indecision now?

It wouldn't be much of a chore; he wouldn't be getting in deep—and they had stuck out a helping hand, taken him in. Maybe he did owe them something more than just fixing doors and chopping wood and the like—and the boy certainly was far too young to be facing the difficulties they were up against.

A homesteader called Henderson. Hardscrabble outfit down near the brakes, to the southeast. Like as not the steers would still be in the yard. It wouldn't be much to just ride over, throw the fear of God into the squatter, and bring the steers back. Be a good time to tell the man that the days of free beef were over, too—that he'd best keep clear of Jackman range.

Still, one step could lead to more. Rusk halted in front of the bunkhouse, eyes on the loose door hinge he intended to repair . . . He'd sworn a silent vow, one promising never to get involved, to have no part of trouble, either his own or someone else's—and he had two crippled hands to remind him of that vow. No matter what, he'd turn and walk away, he'd ride off—he'd even run if need be, but he'd keep clear of trouble.

But the boy—and April; they were like lambs in a world of hungering wolves. He looked over his shoulder. They were walking slowly toward the house, heads down, not talking, the picture of dejection and defeat . . . Defeat. He knew all about defeat.

Abruptly, he angled toward the barn, entered, and backing the chestnut into the runway, swung onto the saddle. Shortly he rode through the wide doorway and headed for the range where the Jackman herd was grazing.

# CHAPTER SEVEN

It was a fine ranch. Matt Rusk's practiced eye noted this as he rode on through the climbing heat of late morning. Grass was plentiful—thick, rich green, and up to the chestnut's hocks in most places. There were many small groves of cottonwood and sycamore trees, scattered here and there offering shade, and the nearby Ute River seemed to provide source for any number of shallow ponds and sinks.

There was small reason to question Frank Sutter's desire for the Jackman spread. A ranch with such assets, extending from one end of the Sagebrush Hills to the other, and east as far as the eye could see, would, indeed, be a magnificent piece of property—one with limitless prospects insofar as cattle raising was concerned . . . Vast, open range, a wealth of rich forage, ample, year around water—it was Valhalla to any cattleman.

But a place such as that could take strong grip upon a man, come to mean far too much to him—so much in fact that all else paled in consideration. There was a cost to everything, one that eventually must be paid; was Frank Sutter aware of that? Was he the sort willing to meet that cost?

Likely, from what the Jackmans had said of

him. Rusk shrugged . . . Sutter would learn, just as others had learned—just as he had; a price can be too high if a man permits it.

He saw the herd a few minutes later, a couple hundred or so fat, prime beeves, taking life easy around a good-sized pond ringed with grass that shifted gently back and forth in the breeze. They'd bring top price at the market, and be entitled to it.

He halted in a small grove a hundred yards below the stock, remained in the shadows for a quarter hour watching, probing the clumps of brush and stands of trees for other riders. Finally convinced he was alone, he broke out of the cottonwoods, rode toward the herd, eyes searching the soft ground for prints of horses, or men on foot.

Jackman's cattle lifted their heads, gazed at him disinterestedly as he passed, too lazy to shy off. He circled the upper end of the stock, saw where a rider had approached from the east; Clint, no doubt. The boy had swung in around the grazing cattle, and near a clump of chokecherry, had halted, dropped to the ground.

There were other prints there. Two different horses overriding the tracks of two steers, moving west. They would be the rustlers, driving the stolen animals ahead of them. They were plenty bold; from what Rusk could determine, they had simply ridden into the herd, cut out two beeves that apparently looked good to them, hazed them off to the side, and then pointed for a low rock and grass covered hogback rising in the short distance.

Matt followed the definite trail to the ridge, saw as Clint had reported, where the tracks became lost on the firm ground. Climbing back onto the chestnut, Rusk sat for a time studying the country unfolding before him.

On to the west, all the way to the foot of the Sagebrush Hills, the range appeared unbroken, little changed from that over which he had just ridden. To the south the land seemed to run to grass for a considerable distance and then break up. Weeds appeared to cluster thickly on the crest of knolls, and the bright emerald of good grass faded into a gray-green that, in contrast, looked almost lifeless. The red faces of bluffs could be seen, and mounds of rock reared at frequent intervals.

There, apparently, began the brakes—and the homestead of a man the Jackmans had called Henderson. Both thought him to be the rustler nibbling at their shrinking herd. To Matt Rusk, no stranger to such a situation, there was little doubt. It all ran true to form.

Squatters never stole cattle in large batches as did the hard-case rustlers; they skulked about, drove off one or two, seldom more than that, at a time. Wasting no more effort in looking for tracks, he struck off along the ridge for the distant badlands.

He saw smoke off to his left an hour later, veered his course accordingly, and continued on. This would be the poorest section of the Jackman range, he guessed, mostly sand, snakeweed, chaparral and patches of prickly pear and cholla cactus. Several times he routed long-eared jackrabbits from patches of thin shade where they sought relief from the sun, and once a distinctly marked diamondback rattler, buzzed a warning at him from beneath a ledge.

The smoke he'd spotted was curling upward from a staggering, stovepipe chimney thrusting from the roof of a slab-wood and sod shanty. Matt drew to a stop on the brow of a low butte, looked down upon the beggarly structure and its surroundings.

There was a corral in which, surprisingly, he could see a half a dozen fairly good horses. Two dogs, heads and tails adroop, were crossing the littered yard, pointing for the shade of a thin, water starved apple tree. The privy, three small sheds and the house itself, all appeared on the verge of collapse. The one saving feature of the entire layout was a huge cottonwood, evidently nourished by an underground stream, standing off to the edge of the clearing, spreading its protection over all.

He could see no cattle, and the field below, once

under cultivation, was now neglected, barren. *They never learn,* Matt thought; the country was not suited to farming—never was, never would be. He'd told a dozen hopefuls such in just that many words. Doubtless Henderson had been given identical advice—and like those to whom Rusk had spoken, he'd not listened. Now he was starving it out, looking for charity, stealing to keep himself and his family alive, while the once firm land, broken by the plow, was going to dust.

But if Henderson was the rustler—where were the cattle? Matt gave that thought. And why the good horses? What would a down-and-out squatter be doing with better than average horseflesh?

He could have visions of going into raising horses, Rusk decided, could be building up his string by rustling cattle, then selling or trading them for horses . . . But he would have to keep the steers around somewhere, have them on hand for bargaining.

Dropping back, Rusk circled the place silently, keeping well back in the brush and below the rim of the bluff. When he drew even with the front of the house, he again paused, seeing a horse and buggy drawn up to the hitchrack. Five or six small, dirty children were playing in the shade alongside the shack, digging into the hard baked ground with sharpened sticks.

Still no sign of cattle . . . And the thieves had

74

made off with two steers only hours earlier; it was logical to believe the beef would still be in the rustler's possession after so short a time. Could the Jackmans be wrong about Henderson?

He looked ahead. The butte ran on down to level, disappeared into an arroyo. Holding the chestnut to a slow walk, Matt guided him into the wash, and there angled right toward a densely brushed area lying to the east of the Henderson house.

Coming to that point Matt halted, pulled off his hat and wiped at the sweat on his face. It was somewhere past midday and the heat was at its peak . . . It would be hell inside that board shack, he thought, but then the life of a squatter's wife in this part of the country was always hell. Starvation and kids and never-ending drudgery— that was about all she could look forward to.

Abruptly Matt Rusk came to attention. The rank, unmistakable odor of a cattle pen had come to him. He sat stiffly upright on his saddle, nostrils testing the stilled air, eyes probing the brush around him. He could see nothing, but there were cattle close by—he knew he wasn't wrong about that.

Touching the chestnut lightly with his heels, he pushed forward, the sandy bottom of the arroyo cushioning the gelding's hooves, making his progress silent. The odor became stronger. Rusk pulled up again. A moment later he heard the dry clack of horn meeting horn. The cattle were close.

Rusk did not move. He'd found what he searched for but now the old reluctance to implicate himself was again upon him. He shifted angrily, impatiently, spat into the brush. Of all the places he might have stumbled into, why did it have to be the Jackmans'? And what the hell were they hanging onto that goddam ranch for anyway? Why didn't they sell out to this Sutter, move on before something bad happened to one of them—or both? They were being stubborn—fool stubborn . . . He'd been stubborn, too, once, and what had it got him? If he . . .

"Pa—"

Rusk came to attention at the sound of the voice. It was directly ahead, just beyond a thick line of undergrowth. An odd pattern to the branches caught his attention. He looked more closely, saw that it was not a natural wall of brush. Bits of wire, rope, and vine had been used to make a solid thicket.

"Over here, Jesse."

There was a brief run of silence and then the first voice said: "Was just thinking, it'll take a powerful long time to build us up a big string of horses rate we're going."

"Maybe."

"Instead of us grabbing just a couple of steers

at a time, why don't we run off maybe a dozen? Sure won't be no harder to do."

"Be the wrongest thing we could do! You go taking ten, twelve animals at once, and it'll force somebody's hand, make them do something. The Jackmans might even give in to Frank Sutter and sell out . . . But us sneaking off a couple at a time don't stir up nobody. Riles them, mayhaps, but it don't goose them into doing something that'd knock us out of a real good thing . . . Understand?"

"Reckon so, but it's going to take a long time."

"Everything takes a long time, son, you ought to be knowing that by now. The Good Book says patience is a mighty fine virtue. Means we got to go at a deal like this slow and careful like, so's not to upset things . . . Worst thing we could do'd be to kill off the goose that's a-laying us a golden egg."

"Golden egg? Pa, I don't rightly know what—"

"Never mind. We best be getting back up to the house, see what Doc's got to say about little Linus . . . You for certain sure that gate's hitched tight?"

"Yeh, it's hitched. Pa—what we're doing is stealing, ain't it? And don't the Good Book say—"

"Now, you've got to read the Good Book in just the right way, son. There's them that has, and there's them that ain't got nothing, hardly. Only fair one sort of helps out the other. That's the charity the Book's always talking about.

"Now, we ain't exactly stealing—in a way. Sooner or later Frank Sutter's going to march right in, take over the Jackman place—along with everything on it. The cows the Jackmans've got ain't going to mean nothing to Frank Sutter, him already having more'n a body could count in a lifetime . . . So if there ain't any left on the Jackman place, he won't care. Fact is, I misdoubt if he even knows—"

The voice faded gradually, became lost. Matt realized that Henderson and his son, Jesse apparently, had paused to talk and then moved on toward the house. Slipping from the saddle, he tethered the chestnut, made his way to where he could push through the thicket.

A crude corral, well hidden in the brush, lay before him. A trough half-filled with scummy water stood at one end. Batches of scythe-cut hay were scattered here and about. The place had never been cleaned and the stench at close range was overpowering.

Brushing at the clouds of flies and gnats swarming up to greet him, Matt threw a glance toward the house to be sure Henderson and his son were out of sight. The trail was empty, and moving forward, he stepped into the clearing, pulled the loop free that held the gate secure.

Fourteen steers. Rusk counted them slowly.

The brindle Clint had mentioned caught his eye immediately. Again brushing at the hovering insects, he moved in among the stock. Some still bore the Lazy J brand; marks on others showed evidence of having been altered, but the efforts were poor at best and the Jackman brand was still visible.

Satisfied, Matt shouldered a course back through the cattle to the gate, opened it. Squeezing through, he dropped the loop back into place and then returned to the gelding.

Swinging to the saddle, he glanced toward the house, hidden beyond the thick growth. Somewhere inside him a small voice cried: *last chance to ride on! Don't be a fool—get out now!*

He shrugged, a hardness coming into his deep-set eyes, and wheeling the chestnut about, he started up the trail for the shack.

# CHAPTER EIGHT

Matt broke from the stiff, weedy growth that fringed the trash-littered yard fronting the shack and stopped. Henderson and his son, a much older boy than Clint, were hunkered in the shade of the cottonwood, shoulders resting against its massive trunk. At once the two dogs, dozing beneath the apple tree, rushed forward, yapping furiously.

Henderson looked up, frowned, got to his feet slowly. Jesse, reaching for the rifle he had propped against the tree, also came to a slouching, upright stance. The homesteader snarled at the dogs. Both wheeled instantly, slunk away, this time retreating into an opening under the shack.

Rusk rode deeper into the yard, again halted, this time in front of the two men.

"You Henderson?" he asked of the older one.

The squatter eyed Matt suspiciously. "What if I am?"

"Can't see as it makes any difference," Rusk said coldly. "I'm from Jackman's. Came after the stock you've been stealing from them."

Henderson's jaw sagged. He glanced furtively around the yard. "What stock?"

"Steers you've got penned up down there in the brush."

80

A slatternly woman and a portly, middle-aged man in a dusty, dark suit, appeared in the doorway of the shack. The children playing nearby abandoned their activities, turned their attention to their father. All were ragged, thin-bodied, and streaked with dirt . . . Homesteading was not kind to the young, either.

"You're crazy," Henderson said, raising his voice. "I ain't got none of Jackman's cows . . . Now, you get off my property, or by crackies, I'll—"

The homesteader's voice dwindled as Matt Rusk shifted his weight, swung down from the saddle. Ground reining the chestnut, he moved a few steps nearer to the squatter and his son.

"Don't lie to me about it. I've seen them. Jackman's brand's still on them."

"Not all of them—it ain't!" Jesse shouted.

Henderson half-turned, gave the boy a withering look, said, "You shut up, now, hear?"

"All Jackman's cattle," Rusk said quietly. "Blind man could tell the brands've been blotted, and what they were to start with . . . I'm taking the stock back with me now—and serving notice on you—if you're ever found on Jackman range again it'll go hard on you."

Henderson's face was livid. "Goddammit—you can't come prancing in here, telling me in my own land what I—"

"I'm here," Matt said calmly, "and I'm hoping

81

I won't ever have to come back again. Now, I've already told you—I'm taking the cattle—"

"Like hell you are!" the homesteader yelled, suddenly aware that Matt Rusk was wearing no weapon. "Give me that there gun, Jesse! By God, we'll just see who's doing what around here!"

The younger man made a quick, sideward motion, tossed the fairly new rifle to his father. Henderson caught it neatly, but before he could bring it to bear, Rusk was upon him.

Moving deceptively fast for one so big, Rusk reached out, grabbed the weapon by its barrel, wrenched it from the homesteader's hands. Swinging it in an arc, he struck the ground with the butt of the stock, splintered the wood, and then threw the useless rifle into the brush.

"Goddam you!" Henderson screamed, stunned by the swiftness of it all. "I'll get—"

He lunged, caught Matt around the middle, carried him backward, off balance. Rusk tried to save himself, but Henderson, scrambling wildly, forced him into a scatter of loose firewood. Matt went down with the homesteader still clinging to him.

"Jesse!" Henderson yelled desperately. "Get over here!"

Matt heard the hard pound of the younger man's heels as he raced across the yard to aid his parent. Raising an arm, he smashed a blow into Henderson's cheekbone with the heel of his hand. The grip about his waist relaxed. Twisting, he broke free, started to rise, went down again as Jesse leaped onto him from behind.

He jerked to one side, dislodged the younger, lighter man, struggled to his feet. He stepped back, faced both Hendersons closing in on him now from opposite sides. Dropping into a crouch, he moved forward, flat, gray eyes, locked to those of the older man. Henderson halted, uncertainty on his features.

Jesse rushed in suddenly, fists swinging wildly, awkwardly. Matt caught him by the wrist, spun him aside, sent him sprawling, and then resumed his stalking of the older man.

The squatter began to back away, edging toward the house, eyes shifting nervously back and forth. Matt heard a slight scuffling sound, felt Jesse's weight fall upon him again, cling to his back and shoulders. An instant later the boy's forearm crooked about his throat, tightened.

"That's it, Jesse!" Henderson shouted gleefully. "Choke him good!"

Rusk stalled, planted his feet squarely, legs apart and braced. He reached up for Jesse's arm. Henderson, alarm flooding into his eyes when he saw the possibility of advantage becoming quickly lost, bent low, moved in, fists cocked.

"Keep choking him, Jesse!"

Matt's breath was coming in short drafts. The boy's arm was pressing tight upon his windpipe and breathing was becoming difficult. Staring straight at Henderson, watching his cautious approach, he worked his unwieldy fingers about Jesse's forearm, endeavored to lock them. His hands were not as responsive as once they had been, but by wedging the fingers under Jesse's arm, he managed to pull down, relieve the pressure on his throat to some extent.

Henderson was suddenly before him, crowding in through the layers of stirred-up dust, fists hammering. Matt took a hard blow to the jaw, two or three in the belly that brought a grunt of pain, and sent a long tongue of anger racing through him.

Muttering an oath, he half-turned, warding off the homesteader's blows. Reaching up with his free hand, he twisted his fingers into Jesse's long, unkempt hair. Suddenly buckling forward, he catapulted the younger man over his head, sent him crashing to the ground.

Instantly Matt reversed. His left arm shot out, fast as a striking rattlesnake, caught Henderson by the bib of his filthy overalls and swung him half around. He smashed the man hard along the side of the head, using the heel of his right hand. The homesteader's knees sagged. Rusk, deadly serious, methodical as a mathematician, held the man on his feet, drove another blow to his slack jaw.

"Leave go of him!"

The voice was that of a woman, a shrill command coming from the porch of the shack.

"You hear? Leave him be, or Goddam I'll shoot!"

Matt settled back on his heels, allowed Henderson to crumple into the dust. He shifted his eyes to the house. The woman was clutching an old double-barreled shotgun in her scrawny hands. Both hammers, looking tall as a jackrabbit's ears, were drawn to full cock. Hair was hanging down in her face in stringy, colorless wisps, and her thin lips were pulled back into a snarl. There was no mistaking the promise in her glittering eyes.

"Get yourself away from him—hear?"

Matt did not step back, simply wheeled deliberately to where he could face her fully. Henderson lay on the ground, unstirring. A few paces away Jesse also remained prone. The children, silent through it all, continued to look on with slack interest.

"If you've killed my man—"

"He's not dead. Neither one of them are," Rusk cut in, still breathing harshly. "But they will be if they ever rustle any Jackman cattle again . . . You know they were doing that, Mrs. Henderson?"

"Maybe they was . . . What's it to you—you ain't no Jackman!"

"Work for them. My job to stop this rustling."

"Damn rich ones," the woman muttered. "Losing a cow now and then ain't going to hurt them none." The woman shifted the shotgun to her left hand, brushed at the tip of her dripping nose with the back of the right.

"Jackmans aren't rich. Long way from it— broke, practically. Been that way ever since their pa was bushwhacked and robbed . . . Every steer they got counts big with them."

The woman's jaw came forward belligerently. "We got to eat, same as other folks. Can't let the young'uns starve."

"Stock your husband's been stealing wasn't for that," Matt said coolly. "He's horse trading."

"Well, some of it we're keeping."

The portly man in the dusty, dark suit stirred nervously, ran a shaky hand over his sweating face.

"Makes no difference," Rusk said in a firm voice. "It's done with now. If your husband and son—"

"Jesse ain't mine. The mister was hitched to another woman afore I met him—"

"You tell them both, anyway, to keep clear of Jackman range . . . We hang rustlers where I come from. Reckon the rule's the same down in this part of the country. You be sure they know that, once they wake up."

The woman only stared at him from hostile eyes. Rusk turned toward the gelding. From the side he saw the shotgun in her hands swing up, heard her crabbed, suspicious voice.

"Where you going?"

Holding himself rigid, Matt moved on. Reaching the chestnut, he stepped to the saddle. Only then did he shift his attention to her.

"I'm riding down to that pen and get those steers your man's got corralled, and driving them back where they belong."

"You maybe better not, dammit, or maybe I'll—"

Matt Rusk wagged his head. "Don't try stopping me, Mrs. Henderson. You'll have to kill me to keep me from doing it—and I don't think you want murder tacked on top at rustling."

Rusk studied the woman for a long moment, and then kneeing the chestnut, brought him around, and placing his back to the homesteader's wife, rode into the brush.

Melvin Haley, M.D., once of the tree-shaded precincts of St. Louis and the antisepticized halls of Barnes Medical College, but now the sole practitioner in Cabezo, Territory of New Mexico, mopped agitatedly at the sweat collected on his florid face and heaved a sigh of relief. He glanced nervously at Amanda Henderson, still taut, eyes on the spot in the brush where the big stranger from Jackman's had disappeared.

"You can put that gun down now," he said in

a voice as steady as he could manage under the circumstances. "He's gone."

For about thirty seconds he'd been sure Amanda was going to pull the trigger of the old ten gauge and blow the fellow into Kingdom Come with a load of buckshot . . . Took a lot of guts for that dockwalloper to turn his back the way he did, and ride off. One hell of a man, whoever he was. Wore gloves like a gunslinger—yet he didn't even carry a weapon. Didn't make much sense.

He looked again to Amanda Henderson. She was mumbling words, looking toward the door beyond which the sick boy, Linus, was whimpering softly. Turning, she propped the shotgun against the wall, hurriedly entered the suffocating room . . . A minute before she was ready to kill a man, blast him to smithereens; now an emaciated youngster with a case of the measles was her solitary interests.

Shaking his head at the imponderables of life, Haley stepped down from the porch, crossed to Pete and Jesse Henderson. The children, all of whom would most surely contract little Linus's malady within a few days, resumed their playing in the dirt.

The physician stopped first beside Jesse. He stood the best chance of having sustained injury, being sent flying through the air for a distance of ten feet or so to land with a pretty solid thud. The boy was like a strip of whang leather, had hardly a scratch on him. Getting slammed down flat on the ass as hard as he did would have broken half the bones in most men's body—but not Jesse Henderson . . . The good Lord looks out for fools, drunks, children—*and squatters,* it would appear.

He turned then to Pete, now upright, staring dazedly toward the brush where the stranger had vanished, while he moved his jaw experimentally from side to side. There was nothing wrong with the elder Henderson, either . . . Haley grunted, swore softly. He could never understand how and why the human body could be so indestructible one time, so utterly fragile another.

"Goddam him," Henderson was muttering. "I purely ought to go down there—"

"You better forget that—along with any more of this helping yourself to Jackman's cattle," the doctor said wearily. "That *bravo* meant business."

"Maybe so do I. He ain't stronger than no bullet. I take me a gun—"

"You had a gun," Haley snapped. "Better be happy he only smashed it—and didn't ram it down your throat or up some other part of your anatomy . . . Forget it. I'd like for you to live long enough to pay a little on what you owe me."

Henderson nodded genially, continued to work his jaw. Jesse moved off, began to search about in the brush for the ruined rifle.

"Been aiming to do that, Doc, but things are

89

mighty hard," Henderson said. "Now, I aim to sell a couple of my horses—"

"What you told me a month ago when Mary Joe had the croup. What happened to the cash you got from that sale?"

"Well—there was a right smart a things we needed. And Mandy was bellyaching for clothes for the young'uns. Money just don't go nowheres nowdays, Doc, everything being so high priced, and all."

"I know," Haley said, turning back toward the house. "One thing I will say, you don't blow your money on whiskey like some I can think of."

"Whiskey? Me?" Henderson echoed in a horrified voice. "Why, Doc, I ain't never touched a drop—leastwise not since my first wife died—dang her nagging soul to hell. No sir, not a drop!"

Haley half-smiled, said: "One redeeming virtue buried under a thousand not so laudable."

He reached the porch, climbed up onto its sagging, splintered surface, crossed and entered the sweltering room. Amanda was sitting on the floor. She had the boy in her arms, and eyes closed, was crooning softly as she rocked back and forth. Haley paused beside the slab table, picked up his hat and satchel.

He looked down at the pair and a softness came into his eyes, and possibly for the first time in his life not only the true but the actual meaning of the Hippocratic oath he'd once taken, came to

90

him and he was totally disarmed by this example of helpless, hopeless, destitute humanity for which were only tomorrows of sorrow, and then the cloak of professionalism, impersonal and uninvolved, was again upon his thick shoulders.

"Now, don't forget to give the boy his medicine, Amanda," he said firmly, and returned to the porch.

Pete and Jesse were squatted under the cottonwood, morosely examining the shattered rifle. Haley set his bag on the floor of the buggy, pulled the tie rope free of the hitchrack and after looping it in a harness ring, climbed up onto the seat in the stiff, stuffed manner of a man carrying too much weight on the frame nature saw fit to give him.

"When the rest of the children get sick, let me know," he called to Pete Henderson as he took up the reins. "If the Lord's still favoring me, I'll come."

# CHAPTER NINE

It was near sundown when Clint saw Matt Rusk, topping out a low ridge, driving a small jag of cattle before him.

The boy, sent by April to find Matt and hail him in to supper, watched for a full minute before it finally dawned on him what was taking place; Rusk had ridden over to the Hendersons', had recovered some of the Lazy J's rustled beef!

He could scarcely believe his eyes, and then abruptly he thumped his heels against the ribs of the buckskin he was riding, and raced out to meet Rusk. He charged in head-on, almost spooking the stock before he recovered himself and veered away, coming in belatedly from the side.

"Matt!" he yelled, all smiles. "You got back our rustled steers!"

Rusk nodded irritably. He'd been forced to fight the cattle all the way from Henderson's, and he was in a poor mood for conversation—especially after Clint had come near to scattering the bunch.

"Fourteen!" the boy marveled. "That's sure going to help us a lot." He sobered, added, "Wish't this was all that've ever been rustled."

"All Henderson had," Rusk said, flipping the hindquarters of a lagging steer with the tip of his rope. "Others have been sold or traded off."

"How'd you do it?" Clint asked, pressing in eagerly. "Always heard old man Henderson was real mean . . . Didn't him and Jesse put up a fight?"

"Some."

The boy wagged his head in wonder. "You ain't even mussed up—and you didn't have no gun, either!"

Matt Rusk made no reply. Clint, riding alongside, eyes on the big man's slumped shoulders, felt a glow building within himself as he studied Rusk—one pinched out earlier but now revived by this bold, startling feat.

Maybe there was a chance he could make good his boast to Monte Fox and the others who'd heard him spout off in town, after all . . . Maybe he could sort of work things around, pass Matt Rusk off as the gunslinger he'd promised to produce. Certainly this stunt of just walking into Henderson's and singlehanded taking back the steers the squatters had rustled was enough to open folks' eyes, make them sit up and take notice.

If there was just some way to get Matt into town, let folks get a look at him, and at the same time get the story circulated about how he had— singlehanded—pushed old man Henderson and his boy Jesse aside and taken fourteen stolen steers away from them—he'd be sitting pretty . . .

He just had to think of some means for getting Matt into town.

Had he forgotten anything that April had wanted when he went in the other morning? He hadn't, of course. April had made out the list and Larkin had filled the order. He'd had nothing to do with that part of it . . . Maybe he could come up with some excuse of his own . . . He simply had to work it somehow.

"Supper's most ready," he said, "and you ain't had no dinner."

Matt nodded. "Am a mite hungry."

"Figured you'd be. April sent me to find you— was afraid you'd gone . . . Rode out."

Rusk's heavy brows lifted inquiringly. "Why'd she think that?"

"Thought maybe she'd said something this morning that riled you up."

Matt shrugged. "Agreed to work a month. That's what I'll do."

"What I told her! Said a man like you never breaks his word—no matter what . . . How's the chestnut? He all right?"

Matt again nodded, said, "Good horse."

"We'll get the bill of sale made out tonight. You sure got to have that."

"No hurry. Be here awhile yet."

The swale where the rest of the herd grazed was ahead. The cattle caught sight of their kith, smelling also the water and good grass, and broke into a lazy, shambling trot. Immediately Matt swung the chestnut right, pointed him for the ranch . . . He'd had enough cattle for one day.

Clint caught up with him quickly. "You think I ought to stay with the herd—sort of keep an eye on things for a spell? Old Henderson might try—"

"Don't worry about him. He won't be coming onto your range again."

The boy's expression changed. A stillness came over him. "That mean you—that you had to kill—"

"No. Just made it plain he'd best never set foot on Jackman land again or something like that might happen. Don't think he ever will."

Clint settled back on the buckskin. "I see," he murmured. "Sure glad you didn't have to do nothing bad like that." But there was a shade of regret, of disappointment in his tone . . . If Matt Rusk had been forced to kill old man Henderson—in a fair fight, of course—then folks. . . .

"Killing's not the answer to anything," Rusk said in a quiet, distant voice. "Only the beginning to more trouble . . . Don't ever forget that, boy."

Clint considered that solemnly. Then, "But sometimes don't a man just have to—to use a gun—kill?"

"He may think he has to kill another but that's a frame of mind he works himself up into. Finds out later that there was another answer—another way, and that the killing he's done has only made matters worse."

Clint Jackman took firm grip on his courage. He felt he had to know—and now. "Matt, were you once a gunfighter?"

Rusk's wooden expression did not alter. "Once carried a gun. Don't any more."

"Most every man I ever saw does that—pack a gun. What I mean is—did you carry one to hire out?"

"Know what you mean, and if you wasn't so young you'd not ask a fool question like that—not of me or any man. Deserves no answer . . . And far as a gun goes, best thing you can do is forget there is such a thing. Don't ever hang one on your hip."

The yard was before them. April had already lit a lamp, and hearing the horses, had come into the doorway. Clint broke from Matt at once, went racing across the hard-pack, shouting the good news of the recovery to her.

Rusk turned into the barn, dismounted, and led the chestnut into his stall. Removing saddle and bridle, he forked down a quantity of hay, poured a quart of oats into the manger box, and stood for a moment, weary, both hands flat on the big horse's neck . . . The gelding was a good mount. He'd made a fine choice.

Moving back through the opening, he went to

the bench under the tree, pumped a pan of water and washed away the sweat and dust from his face and neck. Then, slicking down his hair as best he could without comb and brush, he crossed the yard to the house.

April, oddly sober in contrast to the beaming Clint, was waiting in the kitchen. He gave her a close look and silently sat down to the table. Clint, obviously directed by his sister to stifle his tongue as well as his enthusiasm, followed suit. April placed platters of food before them, settled in her chair.

"Want to thank you, Matt," she said immediately as if anxious to get it over with. "But you shouldn't have taken such a big chance . . . Cattle aren't worth it."

She wasn't pleased with him for some reason, Rusk saw, although she was making a show of expressing appreciation.

"Took no chance," he said. "Squatters run pretty much the same everywhere."

"Perhaps, but there's always the possibility of one of them—of someone—losing his head and grabbing up a gun—"

Like Mrs. Henderson, Matt thought, beginning to eat. He'd gone through a bad sixty seconds there when he turned his back on her, knowing she had that scattergun pointed at him. The hackles on his neck still prickled when he thought of it; but he'd banked on the knowledge that she

97

knew to pull the trigger on the weapon would only make things worse.

"Henderson had some pretty fair horses in a corral. Think he got them by trading your beef for them, or maybe selling the beef and then buying . . . Could be you could go to your town marshal, lay claim—"

"I wish he had traded them all off before you got there!" April said in a sudden burst of bitterness.

Clint choked, swallowed hard. Rusk, frowning, raised his eyes to the girl.

"Guess I don't understand that."

"Why can't you? Don't you see that we can't afford to stir up Frank Sutter? When word gets to him of what you've done, he'll probably start all over again—setting fires, raiding, shooting—"

"I'll bet he won't!" Clint blurted. "I'll bet he leaves us alone now after he hears how Matt, singlehanded—"

"Never mind, boy," Rusk said in his quiet, undisturbed way. "Expect your sister's right. Usually best to not stir around in a den of sleeping snakes." He nodded slightly to April. "Reckon all I can do now is say I'm sorry. Know that never helps much."

"Well, you oughtn't to be sorry for doing it!" Clint declared hotly. "You got us back a bunch of our steers that were stole from us—and I think you ought to be thanked, not hollered at!"

"I am thanking you, Matt," the girl said. "Don't misunderstand me. I . . . I appreciate it very much—and you can't possibly realize how important those steers are to us. Only—I hope it ends there . . . Something else, I apologize for the things I said to you this morning. I don't know what got into me. Sometimes I think I don't know my own mind."

"No need to say anything. Can't recollect anything you said that wasn't the truth."

April smiled, pleased at his manner of accepting her apology. "Anyway, it's all done with now. We'll hope for the best—and we have fourteen more steers in our herd than we had this morning."

Matt grinned, pushed back his chair. "Was a fine meal. I'm obliged to you . . . Now, about the morning; you mind if I ride into town? Need to buy myself a decent pair of britches."

A look of pure joy crossed Clint Jackman's face. April smiled.

"Of course not!" she said in an indignant tone. "You don't have to ask. You're free to do as you please."

"Long as I made a deal to work, don't want you ever to think I'm shirking my chores."

"We know you won't be doing that, Matt," Clint said rising. "Don't we, April?"

She smiled again, nodded. Clint said: "There anything you need from town, April? I'd sure like to ride in with Matt, show him the road."

"I expect he can find town without your help," the girl said with a laugh. "But if it's all right with Matt, it's all right with me . . . Can't think of anything I need, however."

Clint was barely listening as he trailed Rusk through the doorway into the evening coolness.

"Don't you worry none about what she said—about getting those steers back and maybe starting trouble with Frank Sutter," the boy said in a low, confidential tone. "She don't really mean it—not the way it sounded, anyway."

Rusk did not reply. He was tired and thoughts of crawling into his bunk occupied his mind completely.

"What you done was right. Man has to stand up, take chances when the time comes."

Matt Rusk eased to a halt. For a long breath he stared off into the night, and then wheeled slowly to face the boy. His hands were locked together in that disquieted way of his—palms pressed tight, chafing, rubbing so hard the leather of the gloves squeaked dryly in protest.

"Listen to your sister," he said in a level voice. "Don't go making yourself after me. I'm not the right man for a pattern."

Abruptly he moved on for the bunkhouse, leaving the boy standing there in the half dark, frowning.

# CHAPTER TEN

They rode out of the yard shortly after breakfast that next morning, Matt sitting high on the chestnut horse, Clint, eager and happy on his buckskin.

Little conversation passed between them and no mention was made of what had been said that previous night as they followed the twin ruts winding in and out of the low hills and across the long prairie known as Skull Flats to the better marked road that brought them into the town.

Several persons were abroad as they turned into the end of the street. Clint Jackman felt a quick swell of pride as all turned to look at the big, hard-faced man who rode beside him . . . If only Matt was wearing a gun—then everything would be absolutely perfect!

But from the expression on people's faces, both along the walks and peering through store windows and from doorways he guessed it didn't matter. Just the appearance of Matt Rusk seemed to haul them up short, put a kind of respect in their eyes.

"That the store where you do your trading?" Rusk asked, pointing with his chin at Larkin's.

Clint nodded and together they angled their

101

slow walking horses toward the hitchrack. Dismounting, they wrapped their reins around the bar, stepped up onto the porch. Clint hurried ahead, pulled back the dust-clogged screen door. Rusk, nodding his thanks to the boy, entered, halted.

Clint grinned, took advantage of the moment to throw his glance down the street to the Alhambra. Disappointment stirred him. No horses were at the rack . . . Monte Fox and the rest of the bunch from Sutter's weren't in town. He'd hoped they'd all be there.

"Something I can do for you?"

Clint turned back into the store, hearing Larkin's voice. The storekeeper sure used a different tone with Matt, the boy noted; one that was very polite.

"Pair of britches," Matt replied. "Hard finish. Denim."

Larkin stepped quickly behind one of the counters, dug through a stack of Levi's, jerked out a pair. "These ought to fit . . . Try them on in the back room if you're of a mind."

Matt unfolded the garment, held it to his waist, gauged also the length. "No need. What's the charge?"

Larkin emerged from behind the counter, named his price. "Anything else?" he asked, studying Rusk closely. "Boots of yours've about seen their best days . . . Can give you a bargain—"

"They'll have to do," Matt said. "Could use a sack of Bull."

The merchant produced the small muslin sack of tobacco with its attached fold of papers, dropped it on the counter. "No charge," he said. "Compliments of the house to a new customer."

Rusk looked keenly at the smiling man as one wary of favors, picked up the tobacco and tucked it into his shirt pocket. "Obliged to you."

Clint smiled broadly at Larkin. "He's Matt Rusk. Works for us," he said as the tall rider moved lazily away.

The storekeeper rubbed at his chin. "Know that. Heard about him and that whoop-tee-do he had at old man Henderson's. Doc Haley was there, saw it all."

Clint's smile widened. Telling Doc Haley something, or having him for a witness, was like putting it in the newspaper—better even. He spread the word faster.

Larkin leaned close to the boy, eyes on Rusk's broad back. "Don't he carry a gun?"

Clint shook his head. "Never likes to, but I reckon he will, the time comes when he needs to."

The storekeeper clucked softly. "It'll come, mark my word on that."

Matt reached the door, paused to look back expectantly at the boy. "You ready?"

"Ready," Clint said, and hastened across the

floor. "There anything else you're needing?"

"A plenty," Matt said, stepping out onto the porch, "but there's no affording it right now. Bit shy of cash."

Clint glanced hopefully toward the Alhambra. Of all the times he'd come to town, this would be the one time when Monte Fox and Charlie Heer weren't around.

"Thought maybe you'd like treating yourself to a drink—whiskey or maybe a beer," he said, hoping to delay their departure . . . Monte and the others just might ride in if they hung around for a bit.

Matt's eyes swung to the saloon. A half smile pulled at the corners of his mouth. "Right good idea at that. Been quite a time since I wet my whistle with a beer and all the fixings."

Stepping off the porch, he crammed his parcel into his saddlebags, buckled the straps tight, spun to Clint.

"Expect you're too young yet for a beer."

The boy shrugged. "Mr. Case won't sell me one, that's for sure. But I can have a sassparilla."

"Then come on. Drinks are on me."

Leaving the horses at Larkin's rack, they crossed the street to the Alhambra, Clint savoring each step, glorying in every moment, reveling in the long glances he saw being cast in their direction.

Folks were really looking Matt Rusk over,

taking in his size, that hard, cool set of his features, the black gloved hands. If only he'd worn a gun! But maybe this was even better, he decided as the wish came to him a second time; could be his not packing one made him seem all the more dangerous—sort of like he felt he didn't need a weapon to just walk around town, but if somebody started trouble . . .

One thing for sure. Folks around Cabezo would be changing their opinion of the Jackmans. They'd all be a mite careful now how they talked and acted.

They halted in front of the saloon. Matt stood for a minute taking in the street, the store fronts, his glance missing nothing. To Clint it was the typical act of a careful gunman, sizing up the place, making certain he was familiar with the layout; others would be thinking the same thing, the boy knew.

Rusk said mildly: "Nice town," and heading across the Alhambra's porch, shouldered through the batwings with Clint at his heels.

The place was deserted except for Case himself, standing behind the bar, and an aged swamper cleaning up debris from last night's business. Case, a slightly built man with a full, curving mustache that he continually stroked, and ice blue eyes bobbed his head at Matt, fixed his stare on the boy.

"Now, Clint, you know you ain't old enough to come in here—"

"He's with me," Rusk said. "Wants a sassparilla. Make mine beer. Lace it with a shot of rye."

Case said, "Yes, sir," and busied himself behind the counter. Shortly he produced a bottle for Clint, a thick, crockery mug for Matt.

Rusk took up his drink, looked at Clint, winked, said, "Luck," and downed his beer. He smacked, nodded to Case. "Once more."

The Alhambra's owner poured the refill, placed it on the bar as Clint supped at his bottle. He seemed inclined to voice a question of some sort, but held back. Apparently Doc Haley's account of the ruckus at Henderson's had been very complete.

Finally he said, "Seen you looking the town over. Figure to stay?"

"For a spell," Rusk answered.

"Place is going to grow. Expect we'll get us a railroad through here one day and then—"

Case's words broke off as the batwings slammed inward. Clint flung a glance to the doors, felt a quick rush of delight and excitement. It was Monte Fox and Charlie Heer. They'd come into town after all. He guessed maybe Matt and him had just got there a little early.

Rusk flicked the pair with disinterested eyes, downed his drink and reached into a pocket for a coin. The two Sutter men edged forward

106

languidly. A few steps short both halted. Monte Fox reached up, lazily pushed his hat to the back of his head. He looked Rusk up and down with deliberate insolence, taking in the faded shirt, the worn, ragged pants, the run-down boots. A scornful smiled pulled at his mouth.

"So you're Jackman's wolf," he said.

Matt came about slowly, hooked his elbows on the bar's edge. A slightly puzzled look was in his eyes but there was a hard set to his lips.

"You talking to me, friend?"

Monte said, "I ain't talking to your grandma." He shifted his attention to Heer. "Sure don't look like much, does he, Charlie? Hide a-showing through them britches, boots right down to his socks . . . You ever see anything any sorrier looking?"

Heer clucked noisily. "Don't wear no gun—but he's got on them genuine gunfighter's gloves. How you figure that, Monte?"

Rusk's face had not changed. Clint, gulping the last of the sarsaparilla, took a step nearer to him, shook his finger at Fox.

"You'd better mind your lip, Monte! He'll—"

"He'll what?" the puncher broke in. "Dance us a jig, maybe? How about it, wolf, you like to dance a jig for me and Charlie?"

"He sure don't act like no wolf to me," Heer mumbled. "Was I asked I'd say we ought to call him Jackman's goat."

Case, giving Rusk a quick, nervous glance, rapped on the counter with a bottle he held in his hand. "All right, boys," he said banteringly, "let's don't have any trouble . . . Come on down to this end of the bar and have yourself a drink—on the house."

"Not now, Tom," Fox said. "Got to get us a real close look at this here ring-tailed wonder."

Matt Rusk's features were tightening. A bitterness was beginning to crimp his lips and there was a glowing in his deep set eyes.

"Take the barkeep's offer," he said softly. "Don't know what's riding you, but you'd best drop it . . . I'm not looking for trouble."

"You're not!" Fox exclaimed. "You hear that, Charlie? He's not looking for trouble . . . Why, we figured that's what you was always hunting. We done been told all about how you was coming here to help your friends, straighten us out good. Then right away we hear how you really worked over old Pete Henderson and his kid. We just had to have us a gander at the man who could do all that."

Charlie Heer pushed forward a step. "Only thing—you'd best remember slapping sodbusters around is one thing, but coming up against real men is something else."

Rusk folded his arms, allowed his shoulders to settle. "Still don't know what this is all about— but if you're just here trying to start something—

108

I'm not interested." He shifted his gaze to Clint. "You about ready to go, boy?"

"Maybe he is but you ain't," Charlie Heer said. "We ain't done with you yet, are we, Monte?"

"No, sir. A real big hero of a gent like him. Now, why don't you see if he's got a belly-button just like the rest of us common folks."

"Sure," Heer said and whipped out his pistol. Jabbing forward, he dug the end of the barrel into Rusk's middle.

Matt's arm lashed out in a blur of motion, swept the gun aside. His gloved hands seized Heer's arm at the wrist and above the elbow, twisted, brought it down hard on the edge of the bar. The snap of the bone was drowned by Heer's howl of pain, by the clatter of his pistol falling into a tray of glasses.

There was a breathless moment of stunned silence, and then Monte Fox yelled: "Goddam you, I'll—"

In a single stride Rusk was upon the puncher. One big, covered hand closed over the pistol Fox was pulling from its leather holster. He wrenched it free and in the same single motion, sent it sailing into a far corner of the room.

Whirling Fox half around, Rusk backhanded him sharply across the face, sent him staggering into the welter of tables and chairs the swamper had pushed into the center of the area. Almost lazily, and without even a glance at the moaning, suffering Charlie Heer slumped against the counter, he nodded to Clint.

"What about it? You ready now?"

Clint gulped the last of the sarsaparilla, forgotten in the blast of excitement, planted the empty bottle on the bar and hurried to Rusk's side. His eyes were shining and pride was riding his shoulders like a soaring eagle.

"Yes, sir, Matt, I'm ready."

Rusk turned toward the swinging doors. Behind him Monte Fox was disentangling himself from the chairs and tables, a steady string of oaths rumbling from his lips. Upright, face flushed, he stared after Matt and the boy.

"We ain't done with you yet, mister!" he shouted. "You can goddam bet we'll be coming after you!"

Rusk paused, hands resting on the scarred, curved tops of the batwings. He half-turned, considered Fox coldly.

"Don't try it," he said, and then pushed on out onto the porch with Clint at his side.

# CHAPTER ELEVEN

There were considerably more persons along the street when Matt and young Clint Jackman stepped through the doorway of the Alhambra and into the open.

It was evident that all had expected some sort of violent altercation after Monte Fox and Charlie Heer had entered the saloon. Now, with the appearance of the big, hard-faced man and the boy—and no intervening gunshots—wonder and speculation were making swift rounds.

Glancing neither right nor left, Matt walked to where the horses waited while Clint, extending himself, matched him stride for stride. Rusk's square-cut, sun-and-wind-darkened features were set, forbidding, and to those who were standing close enough when he passed, the brittle glow in his gray eyes was still visible.

Mounting, he waited for Clint to get himself set on the buckskin, and then wheeling about, rode the length of Cabezo's lone street to where it linked with the road west. Only then did he speak.

"They Sutter's men—the two in the saloon?"

The boy bobbed his head. "Monte Fox and Charlie Heer . . . Was Charlie you give the busted arm to." Clint paused, eyes wide, and whistled

111

softly. "That sure was something! Never seen anything like that happen before—and him poking you in the belly with a gun all the time."

Matt turned his face to the boy. "What's this wolf business—Jackman's wolf?"

Clint looked away hurriedly, then screwing up his courage, said, "All my doings, I reckon. They—the Sutter bunch, mostly Charlie and Monte—are always hoorawing me, pushing me around and making fun of me and our ranch.

"Last time I got real mad. Was just the other day. Before I thought I told them April and me were getting us a hired gun to come and sort of look out for us—a friend of Pa's, I said . . . Then you just sort of showed up at the ranch."

Matt's eyes were almost closed. "And now they—the whole town—figures I'm the hired gun you were talking about, that it?"

Clint barely nodded, peering at Rusk with anxious concern. When the tall rider said no more, he murmured, "Sure didn't aim to cause you no trouble—"

"But seems you did," Rusk said wearily. He shrugged as if trying to dislodge the burden which had settled upon his shoulders . . . First the homesteader thing—now this. He was getting in deeper by the minute. "I don't like this much."

Clint frowned. "But you wasn't scared—could see that myself . . . And them both with guns!"

"Got nothing to do with it. Just no put-in of

112

mine. Been a rule to keep clear of other folks' problems. Had plenty of my own—once, and I'm not looking for more."

Clint's features were sober. "That mean you'll be riding on?"

Rusk considered for a moment. "Can't do that, much as good sense tells me I ought. Taking a like to this horse and I want to work my month, pay him out."

Instantly a smile parted the boy's lips. "That's fine, Matt. And I'll bet you don't have nothing to worry about far as Monte and Charlie are concerned. Reckon they've learned their lesson . . . They'll be leaving us alone."

Matt gave the boy a wry smile. "There's a plenty you've got to learn about men—and their pride. They won't let it end there—can't afford to."

"But you showed—"

"All I did was salve my own pride by showing them I was as tough as they are—which was a fool stunt on my part. Should have just walked out of that saloon. Never proved anything."

"They started it—both of them—"

"Sure. They came looking for trouble. I was sucker enough to give it to them. Violence never helps. One thing just leads to another until finally there's a powerful big blow-up and a lot of people get hurt . . . Reason why I walk soft and do what I can to avoid trouble. Figure a man's a fool to mix in."

Clint said, "I know that because you keep telling me. And maybe it's how a man ought to be, but I don't know. Anyway, I guess I ought to say I'm sorry for dragging you into our mess . . . Can see it was wrong, but it all just kind of worked out this way."

They were topping out a rise, breaking into the edge of Skull Flat which lay mostly to their left—the south. On ahead the long, green slopes and low hillsides of the Jackman place rolled gently away to melt into the heat haze fronting the Sagebrush Hills.

"No need to be sorry. Never helps much, once a thing's done. Man makes a mistake, the right way is to face up to it, carry it on his back without complaining . . . This spread of yours—sure is one of the finest I've ever set eyes on."

"Sure is," Clint replied quickly, happy to be on a different subject. "Pa always said we had the best ranch in the county—even better than Sutter's. His is bigger but he don't have as much water."

"Too bad you can't run more cattle. Grass you've got would support a big herd—several thousand head, if it's all like this."

"It is, better even in places. Pa always said this was his second best range. To the north and west is the real good grass."

The hard luster that had filled Matt Rusk's eyes had faded and the corners of his features had softened. He was now just a man—a cattleman, appreciating the beauty and assets of a wonderful country. "Shame," he murmured.

"Sutter's using some of our north range now. Drove his cattle in there, letting them eat our grass. Ought to be run off only April won't let me do nothing about it. She says there's no point to it since we ain't using the grass and it's only going to waste . . . April always wants to be real careful when it comes to Frank Sutter. Plain don't want to rile him, even if we're in the right. I guess, being a girl, she's scared—"

"Your sister's thinking of you, not herself," Matt cut in. "You're a bit too young to stop a bullet."

"Can look out for myself," Clint declared stiffly, almost sullenly. "She won't hardly let me take a deep breath, and shucks, Matt—I'm pretty near grown up!"

A smile tugged at Rusk's lips but he kept it concealed from the boy, deadly serious in his claim to manhood.

"You're getting there," he said, "but don't push it. Comes soon enough."

They rode on in silence as the day's heat mounted higher. Short of noon they reached the lip of the shallow basin in which the ranch buildings were set, and began the long, gentle downgrade to the yard. Matt turned to Clint.

"Can't see as there's a need for telling your

sister about what happened in town. Only worry her."

Clint nodded, frowning. He was going to find it difficult not to relate the incident and tell how the whole town was standing around, mouths hanging open like they was catching flies, looking at Matt . . . And, too, how old Larkin was so nice and polite and all. But he was smart enough to see that it would upset April; Matt Rusk had taken all the sand out of Frank Sutter's prize turkey gobblers, and he sure wouldn't look kindly upon it. April would have a reason to worry.

"All right," he said, "but I expect she'll be hearing about it anyway. Somebody's liable to drop by."

"Maybe not—leastwise for a while. We'll just let it be something between us. That a deal?"

"It's a deal," the boy said.

Matt spent the remainder of the afternoon working around the bunkhouse and the barn, repairing broken doors, patching harness, and in general doing all the jobs he could find. It was good to keep busy, tie his mind up to where there was no room to think.

Clint stayed close to the house and several times he encountered April in the yard. She accorded him no special attention and he guessed the boy was sticking to their bargain and had said nothing to her concerning his encounter with Sutter's men.

The evening meal was a quiet one, and after an hour or so of sitting in the yard, enjoying the breeze drifting in from the Sagebrushes, Matt made his excuses and turned in. He had neglected the woodpile that day, wanted to get an early start on it in the morning.

Not long after sunrise he was up and at it, wearing his new denim britches, and making the early hour ring with the sound of the double-bitted cutting into logs. April appeared in the doorway not much after that, summoned him to a breakfast of bacon, eggs, biscuits, and coffee. That out of the way, and feeling fine and curiously at ease, he resumed his chore. Clint paused on his way to get his horse and make the morning check on the herd, said a few words and hurried on.

The boy was sticking to his promise, and that was good. Likely there'd be trouble but maybe he could keep it away from the Jackmans', put it on the basis of it being a matter between Heer, Fox, and himself . . . That way it wouldn't worry April.

Such depended upon Frank Sutter, he realized. The rancher could leave it as no more than a saloon brawl between hired hands, or he could step in, take advantage of a situation ready made to his liking—if he were looking for a reason to crack down on the Jackmans.

That appeared to be April's estimation of Frank Sutter in general—forever searching for an excuse to harass and aggravate, even to the low level of instructing his crew to torment a fifteen-year-old boy at every opportunity, hoping thereby to hasten the day when the Jackmans would give up.

Thinking back now, and with April in mind, Matt wished he hadn't given in to impulse—or to conscience, he wasn't sure which it had been—and gone to Henderson's after the stolen cattle . . . That had been the start of it all. Worse luck, the town sawbones had to be there—the short, pudgy man on the porch with Henderson's woman—that was Haley, he guessed. He'd lost no time in spreading a report of the incident.

Maybe the answer was to pull out now; he could turn the chestnut back to the Jackmans, call off the agreement and get out of their lives before he caused them even more trouble than they already had—besides heaping an unwanted portion upon his own shoulders.

He paused, leaned on the ax, swore softly as he gave that consideration. Goddam trouble to hell . . A man tried to dodge it, keep out of its way, but it waited for him in every town, lurked behind every rock, every bush . . . And if a man no longer had any heart for fighting, there was but one answer for him: run—and run again, and again.

The soft thud of hooves brought him up sharply. A dozen riders had entered the yard quietly, were swiftly locking him inside a circle. One man he recognized—Monte Fox . . . This then would be Frank Sutter and his bunch. A dry breath slipped from his lips as a phrase out of the past came to his mind: *the wrecking crew.*

# CHAPTER TWELVE

"That's him," Monte Fox said in a low, angry tone.

A rider on a blooded, nervous stallion pushed forward in the circle. Dressed in range work clothing that showed much use, he was a tough-looking, well-built man somewhere in his mid-forties. He had brick-red hair, and small, light blue eyes that appeared to be steel points.

"I'm Frank Sutter," he said in a flat, inflexible way. "You this here wolf the Jackmans have hired?"

Matt Rusk returned the rancher's pushing stare, continued to lean on the ax handle. He saw Sutter's gaze drop, come to rest on his gloved hands.

"I work here," he replied.

Sutter half-turned, touched Fox with a sneering look. "A goddammed cripple! Look at them hands—and you and Heer let him push you around."

Monte squirmed. "Sure don't slow him down none."

The rancher spat, came back to Rusk. "What happened to them paws of yours, mister? Somebody take it in mind to end your gunfighting days, give them a going over?"

Matt remained silent, simply waited. Sutter was what he figured he'd be; cold, ruthless, hard as nails. He was no rocking-chair rancher, that was plain; doubtless he could rope, brand, cut, and ride herd with the best of his men.

"Gunfighter not wearing iron means one thing—hands are so messed up he can't manage a trigger. That right?"

"Wrong," Rusk said coolly.

"Wrong—what? That you can't handle a gun or you're not a gunfighter—or both?"

"Both."

Sutter laughed, a dry, mirthless sound. "Some of them fingers of yours look like they're sticking straight out—stiff as pokers . . . You ain't ever going to do much good with them, that's for sure . . . But can't see as that's here or there. What I come for is to tell you to vamoose—get the hell out of the country . . . Now."

Rusk's features registered their first change. His jaw drew into a hard, white line. His eyes narrowed perceptibly.

"*You're* telling me?" he said. "Just who the hell you think you are?"

"Know who I am," Frank Sutter said blandly. "Also happens I know what I can do—and one thing's sure, I'm running this valley. Smart thing for you to do is saddle up and ride—pronto."

Rusk's level gaze never strayed from the rancher's face . . . It would be the smart thing, all right—move on, pull out of this now before getting more deeply involved. A man can't beat the Sutters . . . He'd learned that up in Montana . . .

"You listening to me, cripple? You don't take my advice like as not you'll end up in a hell of a lot worse shape than you are now."

A calmness came over Matt Rusk; a strange, unfamiliar relief that seemed to free the tautness in his mind, break the tight bands that for so long had gripped his heart, his lungs—his entire being and restricted his every thought and action. Faintly, as if from a distance he heard himself speak. "Aim to stay. Like it here."

Frank Sutter shrugged. "Sort of had a hunch you'd feel that way. You gun-happy saddle-warmers never seem to learn. Guess I'll just have to start you on your way . . . Shake out your ropes, boys."

Matt drew himself up, lifted the heavy double-bitted ax. Several of Sutter's men unhooked their lariats, began to shape loops.

"All right, all right," the rancher said impatiently. "Don't take all day."

Two of the ropes snaked out at once. Matt knocked one aside. The second hung on his shoulder. He grabbed it quickly, threw his weight against it. The puncher at the other end, caught off balance, tumbled to the ground in an awkward sprawl.

Sutter swore roundly. Other loops reached out for Rusk. He felt one settle about him, snatched it, threw it off, but before he could dislodge another, a third had dropped around his ankles. He tried to kick free, felt others encircle him, tighten. Abruptly he found himself pinned, arms clamped to his sides, feet jammed together as the three riders holding him, pulled back into different directions.

Sutter said: "Dust him off!"

Immediately Matt was yanked off his feet as the punchers spurred their horses. He hit the ground hard, bounced, felt rocks, weeds, exposed roots dig into his body as he was dragged around the edge of the yard.

Dust filled his mouth, his eyes, clogged his nostrils. Branches whipped at his face, scratching, slashing. His shoulder came up against something solid, and stronger pain overrode that already stabbing at him in a dozen or more places. His senses flagged as his head glanced off something unyielding; and then again he was motionless in the center of the yard, flat on his back, staring up at Frank Sutter through a yellow haze. The rancher was grinning.

"Just wanted to prove I wasn't joshing you none. Mean what I say. Always have."

Matt Rusk fought off the mist that clouded his brain, struggled to a sitting position. The cynical, apathetic indifference that had governed him for so long seemed to have receded into the back of his mind; pure hatred now gleamed in his eyes.

"The hell with you, Sutter," he snarled, spitting dust.

The redheaded rancher scratched at his jaw. "Seems he needs a bit more proof, boys. Still talking mighty big . . . Wait," he added as the punchers began to back off their horses, pull taut the ropes again. "Let's take a look at them hands of his'n. I'm real curious . . . Bruner, get down there and peel off them gloves."

A huskily built, dark man dropped from his saddle, trotted to where Rusk sat. As he drew near Matt rolled over, struck out with his feet.

Bruner jerked away, a curse ripping from his lips. "Tighten up on them lassos!" he yelled.

The riders backed the horses a few steps, dragging Rusk over, pinning him flat once more. Bruner knelt down, loosened the laces in Matt's gloves, stripped them off and stepped to one side. Frank Sutter rode in closer, an eager look on his leathery face. He moved his head admiringly.

"Now, that's what I call a right good job of mashing up a man's hands," he said, taking some kind of sadistic pleasure from the sight.

Only the thumbs were intact. The fingers were gnarled, misshapen, nails on most either missing or growing at odd angles. The skin was a pasty, gray color splotched with angry red slashes. No

124

knuckles were discernible, only lumpy, crushed bone.

"Yes, sir, a real fine job," Sutter continued. "Somebody sure must've been pissed off at you, cowboy . . . Don't see how you can even hold anything—like that ax you've been swinging."

"It's the thumbs," someone volunteered. "Long as a man's got thumbs he can do plenty. Now, was we to bust them up good, he'd sure never be holding nothing again."

"Can't do that, Henry," Sutter said, winking. "Few things a man just has to have his hands for."

"Why don't we break his arm, like he done Charlie? Both of them—or we could bust up his legs."

"And have him laying around here while things are mending?" Sutter said, shaking his head. "I'm wanting him out of the country—not roosting here for the next couple or three months." He paused, looked down at Rusk's sweating, dust-covered face.

"Tell you what, Mister Gunfighter, I aim to be right nice to you. I'm setting you on your horse, and then we're all taking a ride to the end of the valley—escort like, the way it was in the Army.

"We get there, I'm turning you loose—and you'd better keep right on going, understand? You take a notion to come back and I'll be waiting for you. Know what'll happen then? I'll have the boys pull off them boots you're wearing, and then we'll take a gun butt and fix you up a pair of feet to match them hands . . . How's that sound to you?"

Rusk only stared at the rancher through hating eyes.

"Well, you'd better believe it, because, far as I'm concerned, it's a promise—and a promise is something I always keep . . . That clear?"

Matt struggled against the ropes cutting into his arms and legs. His face was bleak, his voice harsh, and all the old, haunting fears and bitter memories of Montana had melted into the past, leaving him at last, unfettered. He shook his head, spat.

"Go to hell, you sonofabitch," he grated.

April Jackman did not hear Sutter and his men ride in. She was in the south end of the house tidying up Clint's room, and the first indication she had of the rancher's presence was when she finished and went into the kitchen to start making preparations for the noon meal.

She heard voices then, glanced out the window. Three men had ropes on Matt Rusk, were keeping him flat on the ground while Dave Bruner bent over him and pulled the gloves from his hands. That done, Frank Sutter moved in, smiling, leaned down for a better look and made some remark.

Horrified, frozen, fearful of doing anything that would further antagonize the rancher, April watched the tableau in the yard in silence, barely hearing what was being said. But she caught enough words to realize that Matt was being threatened, actually ordered to leave the country under promise of dire consequences should he refuse.

He ought to go . . . She hoped he would go . . . It would be better for everyone—for him, for her and Clint. Matt had made it plain he wanted to avoid trouble; something had occurred in the long distant past that scarred him deeply, changed him, turned him into less than a whole man . . . She could understand that. The time always comes when the constant battle against hopeless odds gets to be overwhelming, and the determination to just lean back, ride along with the wind, offer no disturbance, is easy to accept.

It wasn't a decision of courage, she knew that. Weakness, even, but who cares about that? What difference does it really make? Better to be alive and a loser—than dead.

Maybe Clint would never see it in just that light; he could even hate her for feeling the way she did in her struggle to protect him, but he didn't really understand, didn't realize what it meant to fight against a man like Frank Sutter . . . She knew—and maybe someday he'd admit that what she did was best.

Only it was hard to accept, hard to stand by and let yourself be pushed around, see your pride ground into the dust. She should fight—let Clint fight despite his age, if he wanted to—and like their father had always taught them to do . . . But it hadn't really done him any good now, had it? He was dead and a dead man enjoys nothing except peace, and all the things he died for are wasted as far as he is concerned.

*Listen to him, Matt! Go on. Ride out. Don't get hurt on our account. Go your way—and forget everybody else. I won't blame you for it's the best way when you come right down to it. Look out for yourself—that's the rule. Not a satisfying way of life, but a sensible one—and a safe one. Forget the world. Forget the people in it. Live only for yourself.*

But something was changing in Matt Rusk as he lay helpless there in the yard. Despite whatever it was that stood dark and forbidding in his background, it seemed no longer to be having its influence over him. There was a defiance to him as he stared back at Sutter, hurling an almost visible hatred with his eyes at the rancher and the men with him.

A tightness gripped April's throat, threatened her breathing. She was witnessing a birthing, a metamorphosis. Matt Rusk had thrown aside his cloak of bitter indifference, was again becoming a part of the world in which he lived;

he was finding himself . . . And he just might die. He'd fight Frank Sutter to his last drop of blood—even if she refused to accept his help in her problems—for his own satisfaction. The only way Sutter could beat him would be to kill him.

"Go to hell, you sonofabitch!"

At the sound of Matt Rusk's strong, harsh words, April Jackman knew she could not stand by her own convictions. A change had come over Matt—a change was also coming over her. Wheeling, she ran to her father's room, snatched up the rifle standing in the corner. Levering it partly she made certain a cartridge was in the chamber, and returned swiftly to the kitchen. She hadn't fired the weapon in months, but it was a familiar gun and she had learned, at her father's insistence, to use it well.

Halting at the window, she slid the sash quietly to one side, laid the barrel across the sill. The men were dragging Matt to his feet. Taking careful aim on Frank Sutter's sweat-stained hat, she pressed off a shot.

At the report the rancher's headgear flew off, sailed crazily to the ground. There was a ragged tear in the crown. Sutter yelled his surprise, as did some of the riders with him.

"I've got this gun pointed at your heart, Frank Sutter," April called in a clear voice. She felt good, almost exalted. "I hope I won't have to pull the trigger. Now, tell your crew to turn Matt loose."

The rancher, red hair stringing down over his forehead, shielding his eyes with one hand against the streaming sunlight, brought his shying horse around to face the house.

"Put that goddam gun down, girl, or—"

"I'm counting to three," April said and levered the rifle.

The metallic click of the action brought instantaneous response. Sutter threw up his hands in a gesture of compliance.

"All right—turn him loose!"

Bruner, still on the ground, stepped forward, warily jerked slack into the loops, allowed the ropes to sag, drop to Rusk's feet, and then hurriedly returned to his horse.

Matt stepped clear of the coils, reached down and picked up his gloves, hard glance never once leaving Frank Sutter.

"Now—get out of here!" April ordered.

One of the punchers leaned over, scooped up the rancher's hat, passed it to him. Sutter pulled it on savagely, ignoring the blackened rent, and kneed his horse in close to Rusk.

"Nothing's changed," he snapped. "You've got two days—till the end of the week—to pull out. Better not be here after that."

Jamming spurs to his horse, he wheeled, led his men from the yard.

# CHAPTER THIRTEEN

Rusk watched Sutter and the others ride off in grim silence. Anger was hammering at him and it was on his lips to reply: *I'll be waiting,* but that was for April to say.

He dropped his eyes to his misshapen hands, and for several long moments considered them while the past came flooding back once more, rebuilding the dark memories, shaping again the shadows, but not quite having its way with him as once it did. And then as the sound of a door slamming came to him, he roused quickly, began to draw on his gloves.

"Are you hurt?"

He came about at April's question. Her eyes were not upon his dirt-streaked face but upon his hands, and he saw a faint tremor pass through her as he finished drawing on the leather coverings.

"Not specially," he said and made a gesture at his leg. "Got my new britches tore a little . . . Want to thank you for speaking up with that rifle."

The tension seemed to break in the girl. She smiled. "I can fix that easy with a needle and thread. I'm asking about all those scratches—and the places where you're bleeding. If you'll come inside—"

"Not necessary," he replied, almost impatiently. "Got worse falling off a horse. Little soap and water'll take care of them." He raised his glance, stared off into the north. Sutter and his men were out of sight, lost beyond the smooth, grassy hills. "Expect I've brought you the trouble you've been trying to dodge."

April's voice was careful. "Could be it would have come anyway."

He shook his head. "No, it's me. If I hadn't slapped those hired hands of his around yesterday, he wouldn't have."

April revealed her surprise. "What hired hands?"

He said, "Let it go. Means nothing now. Important thing is that if I hang around, Sutter'll be back, and next time he won't hold off on anything. You sort of cut him to the quick, putting a hole in his hat the way you did."

Rusk paused, thinking of that while a small smile played at the corners of his mouth. Then, "Haven't worked enough to pay for the chestnut, but if you'll trust me I'll send back the money soon's I land a job."

April looked down, bit at her lip. "That mean you want to move on—"

"Best for everybody, especially you and the boy."

She lifted her face to him. "Maybe I thought that once. I've changed I guess, and things are different. Seeing you laying there in the dust giving Frank Sutter as good as he gave in front of all those men did something for me. Feel now I owe—"

"Don't let things get all mixed up in your mind," he cut in. "I didn't do anything—and you owe me nothing, April."

"Don't actually mean you so much—I guess I mean Clint—and myself. I got my mind in a rut somehow, after Papa was killed, a rut I think I hoped I could hide in and someday pull in over Clint and me."

Matt Rusk smiled grimly. "A feeling I've been close friends with for quite a spell—five years in fact."

"But you've climbed out of it now, Matt, whether you realize it or not . . . And you've pulled me with you."

He was staring at her, an odd, eager light in his eyes. But his voice was utterly calm when he spoke.

"Can happen, I guess."

"Of course it can—and it has!" she exclaimed with a show of impatience of her own. "And if you think I'm going to let you ride out after I went to all the trouble of shooting Frank Sutter's hat off his head, why—you can just guess again!"

A smile cracked Matt's lips. April glared at him angrily for several moments and then burst into a laugh. She sobered quickly.

"I mean it, Matt," she said.

He dug into his pocket, produced the sack of tobacco he'd gotten from Larkin's. Selecting a sheet of the thin paper, he tapped out a trench of yellow grains, rolled a perfect cylinder between a thumb and stiffly upright forefinger. Studying the product, he shook his head.

"Maybe you'd better be the one to do some thinking, April. Sutter's not the kind to ever back off—quit."

"Neither am I!" she flared. "Clint and I were both taught to be that way—and Sutter's in the wrong."

"Don't necessarily mean he can't win. Men in the wrong win out pretty regularly."

Her mouth was set to a stubborn line. "Perhaps, but there is some strength in being right, no matter what you say."

"No doubt, but it's mighty poor protection against a bullet—or a posse. You've got a fine ranch here, worth more'n most. Sutter knows that and about the only thing that'll keep him from getting his hands on it—is being dead."

She watched him dig out a match, scrape it into a flame and light his cigarette. "I know that," she said with a sigh. "If there was only some way I could keep going—keep him from forcing us out."

Rusk exhaled a small cloud of smoke, looked at her keenly. "You mean that—for sure?"

"Of course I do! It's our home—our land, and today I got a look at what happens when people just give up and don't fight to hold on to what's theirs—they just make men like Frank Sutter greedier, make them want to hog more—everything . . . Why?"

Matt puffed slowly on his cigarette, removed it from his lips, held it to one side and motioned toward the bench beneath the nearby cottonwood tree. They crossed, sat down, Matt still thoughtful. Abruptly he threw the cigarette to the ground, faced her.

"Now, I won't say this in front of the boy, only to you since you're the one looking out for him, and I won't make your job harder—but there is a way you might get your ranch started again if you're willing to make the try . . . Be on a small scale."

April Jackman stirred uneasily, as if arousing from a dream—a dream in which all things had appeared bright and hopeful and courage came easy. He realized that and spared her nothing.

"Means out and out bucking Sutter. Raids, fires, guns—everything."

All the doubts and fears were upon her again suddenly, showing in her eyes, in her face, in the tight drawn line of her lips. For a long breath she seemed about to give in to those fears, and then she straightened.

"I don't care. I think I should do it—for Clint's

sake. The ranch is ours and it's wrong not to fight for it . . . It would be like—well, cheating him." She paused, brushed at a lock of stray hair falling down upon one cheek, said, "But how can we do anything? We've no money, not enough cattle to even fool with . . ."

"Won't need money," Rusk said. "Only grass. I'll tell you how it's done, you think it over tonight—talk to Clint about it if you think it's wise—"

"I know what he'll say right now!"

Matt grinned. "Quite a boy," he murmured. "Here's what you can do—you can lease out. Quite a bit of it being done nowadays. Ranchers, especially the syndicate people over in Texas, are always looking for grazing rights. They're in the cattle business in a big way and I've not bumped into one yet that wasn't needing range."

"I—I don't want to sell—"

"No selling to it—lease. That means they drive their cattle, however many you may decide on, onto your land. You let them graze and fatten for a certain time, something you agree on, too, and they pay you for that right."

"How much?"

"Depends on the range. You've got plenty available, all of it prime country—plenty of good grass and permanent water . . . But I wasn't thinking about your collecting in cash. I figure you'd be smart to take your pay in cattle."

April's brow furrowed. "Why? With cash we could go out, buy stock."

"Sure, but thing is you'll get a lot better deal if you'll take your fee in steers. Cash is always hard to come by, even where the big outfits are concerned. They've always got lots of cattle.

"For another reason, you'll get your steers first off, right when their herd's driven in. You won't have to wait several months for your pay to come through."

April was hesitant, almost reluctant to ask her next question. "How much do you think we can get?"

"Figuring you'll take cattle, the usual pay-off is ten percent of the herd that's to be grazed . . . They move in a thousand head, your cut's a hundred . . . My idea is to holler for a bigger percentage."

"A hundred steers," April said in a disbelieving tone. "That's way more than I expected."

"Percent varies, of course. Your range is better'n average. I'd ask twenty percent, settle for less. I figure I can convince the man I'm thinking about that your range is worth it."

April was staring at him. "Matt—you really think you can do that? You know somebody—a syndicate—that might be interested?"

He nodded. "Also happen to know things are plenty dry over in Texas. Prime range will look like pure gold to them."

"We've got a lot of that . . . How much of a herd can we handle?"

"Easy two thousand head. That'll leave you the whole south pasture, below the ridge, for your own beef."

April was calculating, her eyes bright. "Two thousand head—and if you can even get them to pay fifteen percent—that'll mean three hundred steers . . . With what we've still got, our herd would jump to five hundred right off! Oh, Matt, do you think you can work it?"

"Nothing's ever for dead certain except the graveyard, but I figure I can . . . Big thing is whether you want to go ahead. Don't forget Sutter. Will mean a showdown with him for sure."

Her face was quiet, solemn. "It will come now anyway—I won't be afraid if you're here."

"I'll be here," he said quietly, "long as you want it . . . Came to me when I was laying there in the dust that a man can run away from nothing—peace or trouble. Catches up no matter where he goes or what he does."

"I—we need you," April said in a simple, flat assurance, and then hurriedly added: "What about Sutter's cattle? They're on our north range—and that's where we'll put a herd if you can make a deal."

"Sutter'll have to get his beef off," Matt said. "Job for me to handle. And once the syndicate's herd is on the ground, they'll take care of things. Sutter won't try moving back."

April moved her head back and forth slowly, wonderingly. "It all seems so good—too good, in fact, to be true . . . If we could do this leasing for maybe three years, and if we could have a good calf drop, why we'd soon build up to a thousand head!"

"Three years lease-out is about all you ought to figure on. Range will be pretty well grazed over by then, and like you said, your own herd will be up to a fair tally. You'll probably need all the grass you'll have."

"I only wish I had those kind of worries—more cattle than I have grass for. Would be a change."

"Few good years and you'll probably be looking at that kind of trouble. But Sutter's what we have to worry about now. He won't want you getting the ranch back in shape—but everything has a price and I guess he's it far as you and your brother are concerned . . . Question you've got to answer is—do you pay it?"

"I—"

"Don't make up your mind now. Think it over. Sleep on it. Talk it over with Clint if you feel like it, then let me know in the morning." He looked away, eyes reaching out to the Sagebrush Hills. "Don't let me muddle up your common sense. You decide it's not worth the risk—the fight, it'll be jake with me. Can still find myself a job in Texas if you'll trust me for the chestnut."

"I've already answered that. I told you I want you to stay."

"Sure, but you've got to work this out on a practical basis—what's best and safest for you and your brother—think about it along the lines you were when I first got here . . . What I'm trying to say is, don't let me being here cause you to feel you can take on the whole world and lick it." He paused, brushed at the sweat on his face. "Truth is, I'm not even sure—if it comes to a fight—guns—"

"I'm sure," April said quietly. "There's no doubt in my mind at all."

He shook his head, and that impatience that gripped him at times when he found it difficult to make others see his point, sharpened his words.

"Anyway—think about it good. Figure the odds. Then let me know in the morning . . . There a telegraph office in town?"

"Yes. In the hotel lobby."

"Good. You decide you want to go ahead, I'll ride in, send a telegram message to the syndicate's office in Fort Worth. Friend of mine's the head man. They run most of the cattle in the Panhandle."

"Will you—we know right away if they're interested?"

"Should get the answer while I'm waiting there."

Again April sighed, smiled. "It all seems so good, Matt . . . Having cattle again, a real herd—stock to sell in the spring like we used to. We'll be able to fix things up, do some of the things we once did, and stop living, well, on charity."

"Is charity—Frank Sutter's charity," Matt said, a hardness in his tone. "Way it looks to me he was just letting you and Clint stay here, sort of rot away until he found it right to move in, take over. You get no help, no anything—not from anybody unless it's all right with him . . . That's the worst kind of charity."

"If you can make a deal for us, that will end. Matt, so much depends on it—all of a sudden!"

"Things have a way of coming to a head," Rusk said. "And it'll all work out fine. No reason why this can't become one of the best ranches in the Territory. Fact is," he added glancing again to the direction in which Sutter had ridden, "I've got a sort of special reason to see that it turns out that way."

"It can," the girl said, "if you'll stay and help us. We'll need you, Matt."

He bobbed his head. "Be here long as you want . . . Now, I've got some choring to do. Getting behind. You wallow all we've been talking about around in your head, let me know what's what in the morning."

"Think I know right now, but I'll do as you say."

Rusk grinned, touched the brim of his hat and started for the pump and washbench beyond the bunkhouse. The first thing he must do is wash off the dust he'd collected when Sutter's bunch had dragged him around the yard.

"Matt . . ."

He halted, turned to face April.

"With things the way they are—with Sutter, I mean, don't you think you ought to have a gun of some kind?"

He was silent for a long moment, said finally: "We won't be hearing from him for a couple of days. Gave me until the end of the week to get out of the country—so there's no need."

"But I'd feel better if you had a weapon handy. You can take my rifle—"

He shrugged, as if surrendering. "Shotgun'll be better. Has a big trigger guard. Expect I'll need all the room I can get if I try to use these fingers."

She nodded, understanding. "There's one in Papa's closet. I'll have Clint put it and some shells in the bunkhouse. Should have it handy in case of unexpected trouble."

He watched her, trim and graceful, move off, and then continued on toward the washbench . . . If and when the moment came that he would be forced to use a gun, would he be able to measure up? Angrily, he broke off the disturbing thought . . . It was a question he would find no answer to until that exact fragment of time presented itself.

# CHAPTER FOURTEEN

Shortly after sunrise Matt Rusk was astride the chestnut and on his way to town. April's thinking had not changed; if anything, she was more taken by the lease idea after mulling it over for a night than she had been when he first outlined the plan to her. And young Clint—there was no way he could restrain his soaring hopes and enthusiasm.

It would work out fine, Matt was convinced—just as he was also convinced there would be trouble with Frank Sutter. That gave him grounds for worry. He couldn't expect to be with the girl and her brother every hour of the day; there would be times when he'd be with the herd, or in town, or elsewhere on the range, and at such moments the two would be unprotected.

Not that April and Clint were unwilling or unable to fight; the opposite was true, but they would prove no match for Frank Sutter's bully-boy riders, and that realization laid a strong disturbance upon him. Best he try and locate a couple of men to hire on, have around the place. They'd have to wait a bit for their first wages but if he talked hard enough, bragged up April's cooking, he just might sell somebody on a job.

Meanwhile, he'd fort up the house. Put heavy shutters on the windows, reinforce the doors.

And while he was absent he'd instruct them to stay inside, or at least not to move too far from the protection of the thick walls.

Best he rig up some sort of signal, too, a means by which they could summon him if an emergency arose. Such precautions would only be necessary until the syndicate riders moved in and took over the range. Once that became fact, Sutter would back off; he'd have no liking for a full scale war where his opponents would not be just a girl, a young boy and a lone hired hand, but a half a dozen or more hard-bitten cowpunchers.

Cabezo presented its usual deserted appearance when he turned into the street and pointed for the Ute Hotel where April said telegraph facilities were maintained. When he pulled up to the hitchrack and dismounted, he noted with a wry grin that a dozen or more residents had risen from nowhere, seemingly, were now standing in doorways, at windows and along the board sidewalks, watching him with bright curiosity.

Such caused him to wonder if word of the encounter with Sutter and his crew that previous day had reached the settlement—but he considered it only briefly. There had been no outside witnesses as there had been at Henderson's, or later, at the Alhambra Saloon—and neither Frank Sutter nor any member of the party was likely to admit being humbled by April Jackman.

He stepped up onto the porch of the hostelry,

entered the dusty lobby and halted, throwing his glance around the room in search of the telegraph operator's quarters. A railed-off section, with a counter along one side and in a corner facing the street, enclosed a desk and chair. On a small side shelf Matt could see the brass and black instruments of the communication system, along with a spindle of old telegrams and other papers . . . No operator was to be seen.

He walked on farther into the lobby, halted at the hotel desk. The clerk was not in sight, and he banged sharply on the dome-shaped bell provided for such occasions. Immediately a balding man, steel-rimmed spectacles pushed to his forehead, came through a gently swaying wall of green plush portieres behind the counter, faced Matt.

"Something you want?"

"The telegraph operator. You tell me where I can find him?"

The older man bobbed his head. "Be right with you."

He disappeared behind the drapery, emerged from a doorway to the side and headed across the lobby for the railed-off section. Entering, he picked up a pad of blanks and a pencil, handed them to Rusk. Evidently he doubled as both hotel clerk and telegraph operator.

Matt took the pencil between a thumb and base of a forefinger, put the point to the paper, aware of the man's avid curiosity, and wrote out his message. Handing it to the operator, he said, "I'll wait right here for the answer."

The clerk adjusted his spectacles, said, "Now, let's see if I can read it right . . . Goes to J. Horn, Southwest Cattle Company, Fort Worth, Texas. Message says: Have located extra good range open to lease. Northern New Mexico. Can handle two thousand head. Owner wants beef on twenty percent basis. High but worth it. Answer now. M. Rusk"

The old man pursed his lips, studied Matt. He seemed about to ask a question, thought better of it, and turning to the key, tapped out the message. Rusk moved to a nearby chair, settled down to wait. It could take time as Joe Horn could be out of the office, out of town, even, in which case everything would go into a stall until he could be located.

Ordinarily, however, the syndicate's general manager could be found at the desk in his office from which he directed the operations of the huge, beef raising company. Odds were better than good a reply would be forthcoming within very few minutes.

It required a quarter of an hour. Matt heard the clatter of the receiver, and getting to his feet, returned to the railing, eyes on the operator copying down the message. Completed, the man read it over, added a comma or two, and passed it to Matt.

M. RUSK CABEZO. TY. NEW MEXICO
RESPECT YOUR JUDGMENT OF RANGE.
CAN USE BUT CAN NOT CONVINCE
ASSOCIATES TO PAY TWENTY PERCENT.
WILL OWNER ACCEPT TWELVE?

J. HORN

Matt picked up the pencil, held it poised above a blank sheet of paper for a few moments, then wrote his reply.

J. HORN FORT WORTH TEXAS
RANGE UNUSED SEVERAL YEARS.
GRASS BELLY HIGH. YEAR AROUND
WATER. WILL NEED ONLY SMALL CREW
TO HERD. WORTH TWENTY BUT OWNER
SAYS WILL TAKE FIFTEEN PERCENT.

M. RUSK

The operator read the message, again eyed Matt speculatively, once more withheld any comments, and turned to his key. Rusk sauntered to the window overlooking the street. The town, as earlier, appeared deserted, but he could hear a woman singing somewhere, practicing the scales. A light wagon had pulled into Larkin's lot, and as he watched, a buggy containing a man, a woman and a child rolled up to the front of Doc Haley's office. The man leaped down, gathered the child in his arms, and preceded by the woman, hurried into the physician's quarters.

147

The minutes dragged by. Wiping away the sweat from his face, and turned restless by the lack of immediacy in a reply from Horn, Matt drew back, strolled aimlessly about the lobby, absently inspecting the faded lithographs on the walls, the cobwebby deer heads, the yellowing magazines disintegrating slowly on the central table.

He'd hoped Joe Horn and his syndicate partners would accept the first offer. They needed range, he was certain, and the Jackmans needed cattle; it was only a matter of getting the two together. If Horn and the syndicate refused to go higher than twelve percent, or decided to turn down the proposition entirely, it would be a great disappointment to both April and Clint.

Should that happen, he decided, he'd try elsewhere. There were other cattle companies besides Southwest. It might take a little time to get in touch with the right parties but . . .

The receiver began to click industriously. Matt doubled back to the counter, eyes on the steadily moving hand of the operator. The clacking halted. The operator touched his key, laid aside his pencil, read what he had written and unsmilingly handed the sheet to Matt.

M. RUSK CABEZO, TY NEW MEXICO
AGREE FIFTEEN PERCENT. HAVE
HERD IN PANHANDLE NOW. ESTIMATE

TWENTY FIVE HUNDRED HEAD. WILL
ORDER DRIVE STARTED IMMEDIATELY.
GIVE DIRECTIONS.

J. HORN

Pleased and relieved, Matt clutched the pencil, wrote the answer.

J. HORN SOUTHWEST CATTLE CO
FORT WORTH TEXAS
HAVE DROVERS HEAD WEST FROM
PANHANDLE TO UTE RIVER. FOLLOW
RIVER NORTH. WILL MEET THEM FOUR
DAYS FROM NOW. NECESSARY YOU PAY
FOR MESSAGES. AM BROKE.

M. RUSK

He passed the sheet to the operator. The man read, frowned darkly. "Well, now, I don't know about us doing this—"

"Just send the message," Rusk said.

The man turned to his key, tapped out the code. Finished, he settled back in his chair, pencil drumming on the desk. Shortly the receiver began its steady, terse clacking. The reply was brief. The operator nodded to himself, glanced at Matt.

"It's all right, Mr. Rusk. Your friend's taking care of everything."

Matt said, "Fine," and turned to the door. It

wasn't as good a deal as he'd hoped to get the Jackmans, but it was better than usual. He guessed he should be satisfied—knew April and Clint would be.

Next move was to get ready for the arrival of the syndicate's herd—and that meant getting Sutter's cattle off the north range. Southwest's beef would be driven straight into that area and he wanted the slopes and swales to be in excellent condition. He wanted, also, to handle the problem with Sutter in the best possible way for the sake of the Jackmans' future—legally.

Stepping out onto the porch, he headed for the office of Marshal Avery Kingstreet.

# CHAPTER FIFTEEN

Kingstreet was a lean, older man with shoulder-length, iron-gray hair and a long, down-curving mustache. He had close-set pale-blue eyes and seemed not to notice the intense heat in his small office as he wore not only a coat but collar and string tie as well.

He was standing at the window when Matt entered, had no doubt seen him come from the hotel. The lawman did not look around, simply continued to stare into the street.

"You're the marshal, I take it," Rusk said in a tone not too conducive to a lasting friendship. The mark of experience insofar as the law was concerned, lay like a burning brand upon him, and since the days in Montana he had found it difficult to be civil toward any man who wore a badge.

Kingstreet turned indolently, pulled back the left lapel of his coat, displayed the star pinned to his shirt pocket.

"I am. You the troublemaker that's hanging out at the Jackmans'?"

Matt Rusk's jaw clamped shut. The hell with it. He should have known better than to try and work with the law. But he had to consider the

Jackmans. Taking a firm grip on his temper, he faced the lawman.

"Name's Rusk. There some reason I shouldn't hire out to them?"

Kingstreet settled on the edge of his desk. Sweat had gathered on his forehead but it went ignored.

"No reason, except I don't like troublemakers in my town."

"You talking about that ruckus in the saloon? Was started by Heer and Fox. I only finished it."

"Talking about Pete Henderson. I don't stand for a man taking the law into his own hands. Should have come to me if you had cause to think he was stealing cattle."

"Figured you knew—and was one of those things a marshal can't do anything about . . . Never came here to talk about that, however."

Kingstreet said, "All right, but I'm giving you a warning—I won't put up with no hell raising around here. Now, what's on your mind?"

Matt folded his arms across his chest, looked directly at Kingstreet. "Sutter," he said.

The lawman's expression stiffened. "Frank Sutter?"

"Only Sutter around here, isn't he? Happens he's running cattle on the Jackmans' north range. Lands all been leased and I want notice served on Sutter, ordering him to move his stock off."

A frown now clouded the marshal's features,

disturbing the beads of accumulated sweat. "Leased you say? The Jackman place?"

"A good piece of it."

"Who said they—"

"Jackman's land. They don't need permission from anybody—certainly not Frank Sutter, if that's what you're thinking. Don't own the place yet . . . Can do what they like."

"Of course," Kingstreet murmured, studying Rusk thoughtfully. "Ain't saying they can't . . . This'll be your doings—this lease thing. Seems you're hell bent on starting trouble around here, ain't you!"

Matt shook his head. "Not looking for trouble at all. And there won't be any unless somebody else starts it. How about that notice on Sutter?"

"Nothing I can do for you there. My jurisdiction ends at the town limits. Can't go out into the county on anything like that—wouldn't be legal."

"It is unless the laws of this Territory are different from others I've been in. Something in the books says a town marshal has authority when no other lawman is available."

Kingstreet looked blank, stroked his mustache. "Well, maybe you know more about the law than I do. Far as I'm concerned, it'll have to be checked with the Circuit Judge."

"He here in town?"

"Nope. Due to drop by next week, or the week after."

"Can't wait for him," Matt said impatiently. "Has to be done now. Got a big herd moving in, want that range cleared in plenty of time."

Avery Kingstreet shrugged, pulled himself off his desk and moved lazily back to the window. "Don't see how I can help you any . . . Might be smart for you to stop that herd from coming in— leastwise until things could be straightened out here."

"Not about to do that. Sutter's trespassing and he'll have to get his stock off. Like to handle this according to law so's everything would be to all you good folk's satisfaction, but seems you're not interested in doing it that way. Reckon my next move is to send a telegram to the U. S. Marshal in Santa Fe."

"No reason to bother him," Kingstreet said quietly. "Just step outside and tell Sutter yourself. He just rode in."

Matt Rusk swept the lawman with a contemptuous glance, walked to the doorway. The rancher, accompanied by two riders, was turning in to the rack in front of Gordon's Gun & Harness Shop. He cut his eyes back to Kingstreet.

"Want you standing here in the doorway, Marshal," he said. "Law ought to be a witness to what I have to say to Sutter."

Kingstreet nodded, a knowing sort of smile on his lips.

"Something else you'd better remember—I

came to you first off, asked for your help. You turned me down."

"So you did," the lawman murmured.

Rusk moved off the landing into the street, taking a deep breath of the fresh if hot air. It was a relief to get out of Kingstreet's office—even more to get away from the lawman himself. He glanced to Gordon's. The rancher and his men had dismounted, were starting across Gordon's porch.

"Sutter!"

At Matt's call the rancher halted, came back around. He saw Rusk moving toward him. His head snapped up, betraying his surprise, and then he said something aside to the men with him. Both immediately dropped back a step, fanned out slightly to either side.

Sutter was a smaller man on foot than he had appeared in the saddle, Matt noted idly. And he looked wirier. He wore his pistol low, had the tip of the holster thonged to his leg, gunfighter style. Matt had his wonder about the man then, speculated on the possibility that once that had been his profession; he had the steel hard nerves and the ruthless turn of mind.

Frank Sutter was angry. "You holler at me?"

Matt said, "I did," and let it hang, enjoying the things it did to the redhead. He'd changed hats.

"Had my say to you," the rancher snarled. "Ain't no use begging—"

"Don't intend to," Rusk cut in. Kingstreet was now standing in front of his door. Other men had come into the open along the way, were slouched against the walls of buildings, listening.

"I'm serving notice on you."

Frank Sutter's face went to bright red. Pure hate, further augmented by the embarrassing turn the incident in the Jackman yard had taken, was lying plain upon him.

"Notice? What the hell you talking about?"

"Just came from the marshal's office. Told him you are trespassing a herd on Jackman's north range. I want it moved."

Sutter swore, drew up in stiff outrage. "You want it off! Who the hell are you to be giving an order like that?"

"Put me down as the Jackman ramrod if that'll make you feel better," Matt said offhandedly. "Big thing is, I want that range cleared. You're grazing steers on land that doesn't belong to you. Same thing as stealing grass. Now—get that stock off, Sutter!"

The rancher stared, seemed unable to believe his own ears. He looked around the street wonderingly, laughed in a strained way.

"Listen to that jasper!" he said to the man on his left. "That's Jackman's wolf. He's barking real fierce!"

The rider laughed dutifully, said: "You figure he can bite, too?"

"Well, there's a saying that a barking dog never bites nobody. Suspect it's the same when it comes to wolves—especially the crippled up ones."

Matt stood in silence, anger stirring him only faintly. He'd stated his case for all the good, law-abiding citizens of Cabezo to hear, as well as in front of the legal wearer of the marshal's star; what followed was now strictly up to Frank Sutter.

"Guess you can see he ain't packing no iron," the rancher went on in a loud voice. "Now, that's sure kind of funny—a real mean wolf like him not carrying a gun . . . You ever hear of anything like that, boys? A gunslinger that don't carry a gun . . . I'm wondering if maybe there's a reason—like he just plain don't cotton much to shootings."

"Could be," the puncher on Sutter's right said. "Man sure can get hisself hurt, fooling with guns."

There was a smile on Kingstreet's lips, smiles in evidence elsewhere along the street, although not so openly displayed. Frank Sutter and his men were playing to an appreciative audience. Abruptly Matt's patience came to an end.

"All right, Sutter, you've had your time braying. Listen close—I'm giving you a deadline, same as you gave me . . . Have your cattle off the Jackman range by sundown tomorrow, or I'll move them myself!"

The rancher sobered instantly. His shoulders

pulled back stiffly. "You threatening me, saddle-bum?"

"Take it any way you like. Remember—by sundown tomorrow."

Sutter was immediately beside himself with rage. He took a long step forward, hand dropping to the weapon on his hip. Recalling suddenly that Rusk carried no pistol, and realizing that even he would never get away with shooting down an unarmed man in front of so many witnesses, he checked his movement, came to a full stop.

"Now, let me tell you something, mister," he snarled, hanging his hands on his hips. "Ain't nobody orders me around like that—and there ain't nothing changed far as you and me are concerned . . . Nothing! You saddle up and get out of the country. Them's my last words to you."

"Last word," Rusk said calmly, "is that you move your cattle, or I will."

"You ain't telling me—"

"I am—and everybody along the street's a witness, including your lawman friend. If it's not clear to you, I'm damn sure it is to them!"

Sutter's color heightened. "Why, goddam you, I'll—"

A hard grin cracked Matt Rusk's lips. He looked straight into Sutter's purpling face, nodded, said: "By sundown—tomorrow," and turning away, headed for the hitchrack at the Ute Hotel where the chestnut waited.

# CHAPTER SIXTEEN

Matt Rusk jerked the lines free, swung onto the saddle. Pulling about, he threw a final glance at Sutter and the men standing beside him, and rode on, taking it slow and easy. But he had no illusions where the redheaded rancher was concerned; Sutter might hesitate to gun him down on the street in Cabezo; out on the range it would be a different story.

Reaching the end of the settlement, he cut onto the road leading west. Immediately his view of the town was closed off by a formation of low embankments. He was thus lost to Sutter and all the others, and leaning forward, he roweled the chestnut roughly, broke him into a hard, fast gallop.

He maintained the pace until he gained the first line of higher bluffs lying well this side of Skull Flats, but actually the beginning of the valley country. There, with the gelding blowing for wind, he slowed and looked back. From the lip of the first break he had a far-reaching view; two riders were on the road, coming up fast.

Rusk grinned bleakly. He had known it would be this way. Frank Sutter, smarting under what he considered to be a loss of face before most of the town, knowing Matt now to be a threat insofar as his plans for taking over the Jackman place were concerned—and knowing also that Rusk was unarmed, had dispatched the two men who had been with him to cancel out that threat.

They needed only to get within rifle range to accomplish the chore Sutter had assigned to them, and his riddled body found later would arouse no interest. There would be those who would wonder, having witnessed the confrontation in front of Gordon's, the abrupt departure of Sutter's two men a bit later. But if they connected the two incidents with his death they'd say nothing, simply keep their conclusions to themselves. The matter of personal safety and well being by far outweighed the advisability of questioning the bushwhacking of a drifting cowhand.

Rusk stood up in the stirrups, swept the surrounding country with a probing gaze. He was on the edge of a series of broken hills that extended a short distance to the north, for a much greater length to the south. There was scant growth on the slopes, mostly globe shaped clumps of snakeweed, patches of rabbitbush, cacti and an occasional scrub cedar.

The country offered little protection, but to stay on the road, open for long, straight stretches as it carved its course toward the distant valley where the ranchers lay, was to pose an inviting target for the two men. Immediately he veered off the slight crest, sent the chestnut plunging down the steep face of the bluff, and cut south. Halting again he listened, heard the pound of approaching horses on the baked surface of the road. They were drawing near.

Again he spurred the gelding, started him off at a fast run along the base of the hills. There was no growth of a size to afford cover here, either, and he sought none, simply intended to get as far below the road as possible before Sutter's men reached the crest and discovered he had turned off.

The chestnut ran easily, having no trouble on the slight downgrade despite the unevenness of the ground. Unexpectedly an arroyo slashed across the land ahead. The gelding hit the edge of the low bank, hunched, sailed out to near center. His hooves bit deep into the soft sand and for a brief bit of time he seemed to hang there, frozen in motion, and then his powerful legs were free again and he was hammering on.

A gunshot echoed hollowly through the quiet, hot air. Rusk flung a glance over his shoulder. The riders were on the crest, had spotted him. One had his rifle out, was leveling the barrel for a second try. They were beyond the weapon's range, however, and the bullet fell short. The rifleman tried again, lowered his weapon as if finally convinced, and then both came off the bluff, following the trail the chestnut had made.

Matt turned his attention to the land ahead.

A decided slope lay before him, smoother, but offering no cover. Well off in the distance he saw the grade terminated in a low sink, one in which a considerable growth of brush laid a gray-green band of hope . . . If he could reach that . . .

He looked back just as both men fired, heard the flat crack of the rifles a moment after he saw sand spurt a short distance behind him. They had faster horses than he, that was evident; the chestnut had the strength and staying power, but lacked speed . . . Another hundred yards to the safety of the brush. He bent low over the gelding's outstretched neck, urged him on. The next time Sutter's men opened up their bullets were not likely to fall short.

Suddenly he was down in a narrow wash with the chestnut floundering a bit in the loose footing. Desperate, Matt righted the horse with a tight rein, cut sharp right, sent him pounding for a twisted juniper hard against the foot of the bluffs. He had dropped out of sight insofar as his pursuers were concerned—at least momentarily—and chances were good they would be keeping their eyes straight ahead on the distant, brush-filled swale—and pass him by. If not . . .

Matt Rusk gave that thought, considered the grim results if the gamble failed to pay off . . . So it would end—right there in a sandy arroyo. It fazed him little, actually disturbed him not at all . . . Every man had to die sometime, somewhere . . . Motionless, slumped on the saddle, he waited out the moments behind the gnarled tree.

The sound of the approaching horses grew louder. A man yelled something, words Matt could not distinguish. Abruptly the pair were in front of him, hunkered forward, eyes locked to the brushy basin. Each had his rifle out and ready, anchored under an armpit, one hand clutched about the hammer and trigger mechanism while the other held the reins to his racing horse. In a thudding, creaking blur of motion they swept by—were gone.

Rusk settled back, breathed deeper as he listened to the receding hammer of hooves. He'd been lucky—the trick had worked. They had thought he continued on into the sink, was now somewhere in the tangle of growth choking its depths.

He remained where he was for several minutes, allowing the riders to reach the swale, get well into it, and then certain he would not be seen, pulled out from behind the juniper and doubled back over his tracks to the point at the edge of the wash where he had veered off.

Glancing again toward the sink, he could see a thin dust haze drifting slowly above the rank growth that marked the location of the searching riders. He grinned faintly, thinking of the disagreeable nature of their task, swung the chestnut up onto the weedy path along the foot of the hills and started for the road.

*If he'd been carrying a weapon—even the old shotgun April had mentioned, he wouldn't have had to run, hunt himself a hole in which to hide.*

That thought came to him, brought a frown to his dark features. He shook his head, not liking it; but there was no denying that all the bars were now down, that Frank Sutter would stop at nothing. The rancher's order would be to kill him on sight—and a man had two choices when faced with such—fight back and himself kill—or run.

Matt Rusk felt a heaviness close in upon him, a great and terrible weight that sought to crush him in mind and spirit . . . Kill . . . He'd sworn never again to take up a gun, regardless of cause, of situation, of reason . . . But he had also decided he was through running.

Clint was waiting for him at the gate when he rode up. The boy raced out to meet him, face anxious, eager.

"Did you make a deal for us?" he cried even before the horses drew together.

Matt nodded, grinned. "Pretty good one. Ought to get you three-fifty, four hundred cows."

Clint yelled his delight, wheeled the buckskin on his hind legs and thundered for the house, shouting for April with every stride of his horse. When Rusk reached the yard and pulled up to the hitchrack, the girl was on the porch, listening to Clint's rapid-fire report. She glanced up as Rusk moved toward them.

"It sounds wonderful, Matt."

He brushed his hat to the back of his head. "Tried for that twenty percent, couldn't get it. Came to middle ground—fifteen. Not sure just what size herd they'll bring in. Probably twenty-five hundred head, but they could pick up a few hundred more—small bunches they'll sort of suck in as they make the drive . . . We could get lucky and they'd show up with around three thousand beeves."

Clint whistled. "Three thousand! That'd mean we'd get four hundred and fifty steers."

April brushed at her eyes, said, "I can hardly believe it—that it's happening—"

"Don't bank on the count until they get here," Rusk warned. "I've seen these things go both ways—the count, I mean. But they'll be here, and they'll start out with better'n two thousand head."

"It'll be fine if only that many come—just two thousand. When will they arrive?"

"Not sure of that either. Sounded like the stock they're sending is somewhere in the north Panhandle. If it's the range I worked for them once, it's not far over the line. Take a herd about six or seven days to make it here. They'll be following the Ute . . . Said I'd meet them."

April's face clouded. "Means we'll have to do something about that herd Frank Sutter's got grazing—"

"It's been handled. Ran into him in town, told him he had until sundown tomorrow to get his stock off your range."

April and Clint stared at Matt open mouthed. Finally the girl said: "You told Sutter—ordered him—to move his cattle—"

"Sure. Went to the marshal first, asked him to do it. Figured everything ought to be done legal because of you and the boy. He wasn't interested in helping out, told me to tell Sutter myself. I did."

"In town—there on the street?" Clint asked.

Matt smiled. "Was plenty of witnesses around."

Clint Jackman's eyes were shining, but the shadows of worry again were drawing at April's face. "How did he take it?"

"Can't say it made him happy," Rusk drawled. "But I reckon he understands how things are."

"Did he know then about our arrangement—the lease with the syndicate?"

"Didn't at that time. Probably does now. Doubt if that telegraph operator could ever keep anything quiet. Told the marshal. He's sure to mention it. One way or another, Sutter knows."

She shook her head slowly. "I was hoping—"

"Don't get worked up over it. Sutter just might fool us all. Way it panned out practically the whole town knows he's trespassing on your land, and knowing now that a big herd's being moved in by a Texas syndicate, he could just back off, admit he's licked."

April sighed heavily. "If only he would."

"Can always hope," Matt said, grinning. "Even for a miracle," and turned to go stable the chestnut, but there was little conviction in his voice.

Later that day as they sat in the shade on the porch enjoying the coolness and drinking coffee, April again betrayed her fears.

"What do you think Frank Sutter will do, Matt?"

"He'll move his old cattle that's what!" Clint said positively before Rusk could start a reply. "Reckon he knows now he can't run over us Jackmans—not with Matt here!"

"I hoped—prayed, we'd not have trouble," April said ignoring the boy.

Rusk looked at her closely. She was having second thoughts about the future and its possibilities, he realized, and he would not push her into anything she might regret.

"Not too late to call things off. Can go in tonight, send a telegram to Tom Horn—"

"No!" April broke in quickly as Clint came upright, an anxious look on his face. "I don't want that . . . It's only that we can do so little when we're up against a man like Sutter. He's got everything—men, guns; even the law and everyone else seems to be for him."

"Way it happens sometimes. Was up against the same sort of proposition in Montana about five years ago."

"Montana? You got a ranch there, Matt?" Clint asked with sudden interest.

"Had," Rusk said shrugging. His gaze dropped to the cup in his hands. "Was a fine place. Lost it—everything."

April's tone was gentle. "That what started you drifting?"

"Was the beginning."

"But you've stopped now—here."

He stirred. "Got you to thank for that. Made me see, somehow, that a man can't live inside himself, like he was a box . . . There's other folks in the world."

"All needing someone—"

"Guess that's right. Never believed it before. Figured I didn't need anybody. That's changed."

April smiled. He had come out of the dark shell into which he had retreated—a hiding place in his mind where he had fled after whatever it was that happened in Montana. She wondered about that, but he seemed disinclined to delve further into it. Eventually he'd tell her, unburden himself as all lonely people must at times do, and he'd feel better for it; but she could not—would not—press him now. He must do it of his own will.

"Before the cattle gets here, is there anything we should do—besides clearing the range, I mean?"

"Couple of things I've got in mind," he said, drawing his tobacco and rolling a cigarette. "May not be necessary but I always favor playing safe." He struck a match to the thin, paper cylinder, puffed it to a coal. Exhaling, he allowed the smoke to trickle from his nostrils.

"I'll start on them in the morning," he said, rising.

Stepping off the porch, he glanced to the velvet-like sky, pierced with bright diamond chips. "Nice night," he murmured, and moved off toward the bunkhouse in a slow, easy stride.

Clint sighed happily. "We don't need to be afraid of nobody, April—not with Matt around. He ain't scared of nothing."

"I know," she replied, getting to her feet. And then a small voice within her added silently: *except perhaps of himself . . .* Montana had done terrible things to him; it could have done that, too.

# CHAPTER SEVENTEEN

Rusk slept lightly. Several times during the night he rose, stepped out into the silvered night to listen, glance around the yard. He had endeavored to reassure April Jackman that there was little to worry about—at least for the present—and probably there wasn't; but he was a man who assumed no guarantees, simply acted along precautionary lines.

He was not forgetting the anger he had seen glowing so furiously in Frank Sutter's eyes— anger that would have multiplied tenfold when word of the range lease reached him. Nor was he ignoring the attempt Sutter's men had made on his life—an incident he had intentionally failed to tell April and Clint about since it would only serve to increase the girl's worries . . . Sutter could strike, and strike hard that very night.

But he didn't, and at daylight Matt rolled out, went through the usual early morning procedures, moved then to the woodpile and got in an hour's work with the ax before April called him in to breakfast.

The meal over, he asked for the tape measure the girl kept in her sewing basket, gauged the kitchen window and that in the wall of her father's room. She watched him put down the sizes on a scrap of paper with frowning interest. "What are you doing?"

"Shutters," he said. "Want to be able to block those windows if it gets necessary."

Her face sobered but she made no comment. Rusk returned to the barn, and digging out some two-inch thick planking from a stack of lumber odds and ends, sawed several lengths to form the proper size squares and cross-pieced them together.

From a cast-off leather trace he cut hinges for the panels, and then hung them in their proper openings. A small piece of wood, cut to oblong shape and with a nail in its center served as a simple lock to hold the heavy shutters in position.

"First sign of trouble, get those closed quick," Matt said when the job was done. "It'll turn this kitchen and your pa's room into something like a fort. Be safe, and no chance of flying glass hurting anybody," he added, seeking to imply such was the danger he had in mind. The thick, oilcloth shades could have provided protection from that, he knew, but it would take the two-inch thick boards to stop bullets.

"While we're all in here together, and I'm thinking about it," he said then, pausing near the kitchen door, "we ought to agree on a signal."

"Signal?" Clint said. "What for?"

"Going to be times when I'll be out on the

171

range. Something might come up and you'll want me quick. Fire your rifle twice as fast as you can lever it, count ten, and fire again . . . I hear that I'll come quick."

There was no deceiving April any longer. She faced him squarely. "You're really expecting trouble—of the worst kind, aren't you? Even more than you let on."

"Just if," Rusk said. "Don't know for sure what to expect. That's the reason I'm plugging all the holes. May be for nothing . . . Anyway, it's not for long. Soon as Horn's men get here with that herd, everything will be all right."

"A week off—at least," the girl murmured.

"Know that. Reason I'm getting set for in the meantime. One thing more, want you both to stay close to the house after today . . . I'll keep an eye on your herd. You hear riders coming up, get inside, close the shutters and stay there—no matter what. Door's plenty thick and it's got a drop-bar that'll hold. Use it. If I'm not around, fire the signal."

Clint's features had sobered and there was disappointment in his voice. "I ought to be doing something—helping, somehow. It's our ranch and everything but you're doing all the work, Matt—and telling me to hide."

"Not hide, sort of on guard. Somebody has to be here with April and the house while I'm looking after things on the range."

"But she can shoot and take care of herself. I don't see why I—"

"You're as good with a rifle as April, aren't you?"

"Sure. Better maybe. And I learned to use Pa's six-gun, too."

"That's why it's up to you to sort of take charge around here. Need somebody who can shoot straight—if it comes down to shooting." Turning his head slightly, Rusk winked at April. Relief immediately filled her eyes.

Clint nodded slowly. "Well, if you think I ought . . . What about this morning? You going to be around here? If so, I'll go see to the herd."

Matt thought for a moment. The boy had him cornered, but he guessed there was no big danger yet. He still felt that trouble from Sutter was most likely to come after dark—after the deadline to move the poaching herd had passed.

"Go ahead," he said. "Best you be careful, however. Keep to the trees, Indian style. You spot any riders, don't let them see you—and come back here fast for me. Clear?"

Clint nodded, hurried through the doorway and trotted across the yard for the barn to get the buckskin.

"He'll be all right," Rusk said with a reassuring smile to April. "He stays too long, I'll ride out after him."

"Whatever you say," the girl replied. "A while

ago you said we—Clint and I—were to lock ourselves inside if trouble started, no matter what. That doesn't mean—if you're out there in the yard—that I'm to—"

"Forget me. I'll look after myself. Just get that door closed and barred, and those shutters closed."

"But I couldn't leave you, maybe trapped—"

"Making some arrangements for myself. In the bunkhouse, maybe in the barn loft. Don't worry. Main thing is for you and the boy to get out of the way, be where it's safe . . . And stay in those two rooms. Won't get a chance to fix shutters for the other windows."

April sighed, wiped her hands on her apron. "A lot of bother for trouble you say may not come— and for only a few days."

"I don't mind the work—and it only takes a couple of seconds for something bad to happen. Don't figure to ever get caught off guard, no matter how much of a bother."

*Montana again,* April thought as he turned away, stepped out into the yard and walked toward the barn.

The day wore on. Rusk prepared himself a place in the bunkhouse where he could crouch behind an overturned bunk placed near the window; he chose one near center of the structure where he would have a complete view of the hardpack with the exception, of course, of the area that fronted the house.

In the loft of the barn he dragged together several lengths of planks, and after wiring back the hinged door to the loft's opening, laid a makeshift barrier behind which he could lie.

He made all such preparations with deliberate care, thinking only of their efficiency, not once considering their actual meaning. When he was finished with the loft he returned to the lower floor, stood for a few minutes in the stall with the chestnut absently stroking the animal's neck . . . The overturned bunk next to the window in the crew's quarters, the barricade in the loft—both were of no value unless he intended to defend from one or the other; and to defend meant to use the weapon April had provided.

He had known that, of course, all of the time, but something had continually relegated the thought to the back of his mind, locked it there, unwilling to permit it to come forth, assert itself . . . Now there was no denying it; all the provisions had been made.

Turning slowly, he walked to the bunkhouse, entered, halted just within the doorway. The shotgun with a small, wicker basket of shells, lay upon the bunk next to his. He stood for a time, simply staring at the weapon, and then crossing, sat down on the bed.

He continued to stare at the shotgun, not touching it, his face dark, withdrawn, eyes hollow and far away; finally, with reluctance, he took up the double-barreled weapon, tripped the lock with his thumb. Inserting shells into the dual chambers, he then moved the shotgun and the spare ammunition to the barricade.

He stepped back then, face unchanged, eyes still empty, but there was a sort of relief in his bearing as if, having handled the weapon, he had rid himself of the need for using it . . . But such was short lived; the hour, the moment of crisis was yet to come, and of that he was well aware. He shrugged, spun on a heel, and strode back into the yard, the hope that possibly it would all work out, that it would not come down to a shooting war, trickling through his mind.

Clint returned, reported the cattle were fine, none missing, and that he had seen no riders on the range, either going or coming. After the noon meal Matt caught an hour's sleep, making up for the broken night, and then again busied himself at the various small tasks his eye sought out for him to do.

Supper was early at Rusk's request. At exactly two hours before sundown, he went into the barn to saddle the chestnut. Clint following close, stood to one side as Matt threw gear into place.

"You sure you don't want Pa's six-gun?" the boy asked after a few moments' lapse. "Sure seems you ought to be carrying something."

"I'll get along all right," Rusk replied, finishing the gelding.

Taking up an empty grain sack from the pile at the end of the runway, Matt tucked inside two cans of the blasting powder, used no doubt for stump removal at some earlier time, and that he'd discovered stacked in a rear stall, and hung it across his saddle, placing the cans apart so they would balance and ride properly. Clint's interest picked up instantly.

"What's that for?"

"May need it. Going out to the north range, see if Sutter's moved that herd."

"I'll go, too—"

"No," Rusk cut in quickly. "We're following the rules—starting right now. Up to you to look after April, things around here. Expect I'll be away from the house quite a bit."

Clint's shoulders sagged. He leaned against the wall of the barn, a study in dejection. "You said we needn't worry about trouble yet."

"Said that this morning. Day's gone. Time I get back—and I've found things on the range the way I'm expecting—I figure we'd best be set for anything."

"Find what things on the range?"

"Sutter's cattle still there. My guess is he's not moved them. Leaves it up to me."

The boy's eyes lighted. "That what the blasting powder's for?"

Matt Rusk nodded, swung onto his saddle. "You stick close to the house . . . Depending on you to take care of your sister."

Clint surged forward impulsively, caught at the chestnut's reins. Abruptly he had become serious, worried.

"Matt—you're coming back, ain't you?"

Rusk looked down at the boy. "You can bet on it. I'm pretty good at dodging bullets—"

"Don't mean that."

Matt frowned, puzzled. "What do you mean?"

Clint shifted nervously. "Well, some of the talking I heard you and April doing . . . That you always run from trouble—not fight. That you'd ruther keep going . . . That's what I mean."

Matt Rusk's jaw tightened. He looked away, cut the chestnut around, spurred for the door. "I'll be back," he said, and rode out.

# CHAPTER EIGHTEEN

It was a small herd, five hundred head or so, Matt saw that Sutter was grazing on Jackman's range. They weren't far from the line, being down in a small valley well fringed by trees.

Making his survey from the cover of thick brush along the south end, Rusk painstakingly searched out the riders he knew would be there . . . Two in plain sight with the cattle; one squatting at the edge of the trees to the east, his horse only partly concealed by a large rock. A second rider was a little more than a hundred yards to that man's right.

Some distance farther to the west he spotted two more punchers, and then on the south of the little valley, on the same side as he, were two more men half-hidden in the brush. It was logical to assume there would be one or two additional riders to his right, Rusk decided, since it appeared Frank Sutter, expecting him to make a move at driving off the herd, had thrown a ring around the swale, hoping to convert it into a trap.

Matt, slumped on his saddle, glanced at the sun; it would be down in another half hour, but darkness would not come for double that length of time. He could do nothing until then. Moody, he studied the land before him, shaped up a plan.

It called for getting in close to the herd, to the low clumps of brush he could see a couple of hundred yards this side of the cattle.

It also meant crossing fairly open ground unless—he raised himself in the stirrups, studied the country immediately to the west where a slight ridge was evident. A grunt of satisfaction slipped from his lips as he resumed his seat. A wash lay beyond the ridge, shallow, but it would afford some degree of cover. Hunched low, aided by darkness, he could probably make it to the brush with no difficulty.

The drawback was, he'd be forced to leave the chestnut hidden in the trees, thus putting himself on foot and a considerable distance from the big horse when things began to happen. He considered that for a bit, shrugged; there was no other way; leading the gelding out to the brush in order to have a means for quick escape would be a certain giveaway. He'd have to trust to luck and hope he could make it back in time.

Stepping down, he unslung the gunnysack with its two cans of blasting powder, set them to one side. Then, taking the chestnut deeper into the trees, he tied him securely, making sure the knot wouldn't slip, allow him to bolt if he became frightened.

That done, he returned to the powder cans, sat down to wait. The minutes crawled by with aggravating slowness, allowing too much time for thought—for remembering the way April had looked earlier that morning, the worry he'd seen in her eyes; for hearing again the words Clint had spoken to him just before he rode off . . . They had a right, he told himself half angrily, and brushed it all aside.

He stood up, gazed off into the swale. He could hear but not see the cattle from where he was, and now and then the sound of men's voices reached him. Shortly after sunset a coyote sent up a chorus of yelps, as if greeting the end of day, and then not too much later a covey of plump, top-knotted quail sailed in on set wings seeking cover in the grove for the night.

At full dark he took up the blasting powder, and keeping to the trees, worked his way to the draw. Dropping into it, he hunched low and hurried toward the swale. He neither heard nor saw anyone, guessed Sutter's men were lying low, depending upon him to make the initial move. Or—he grinned bleakly at the thought—they could be pulling out, concluding his threat had been only an idle one . . . He'd be in luck if that was the way of it—only things never came that easy for him.

Gaining the brush, he set the cans on the cooling ground, worked his way through the low, scrub growth to where he could look down upon the herd. It was better than he figured; the cattle were less than a hundred yards distant, a few bedded down, others still on their feet and shifting about restlessly.

The men along the bordering trees were no longer visible, but the punchers designated to remain in full view with the stock, as decoys, had not moved.

Pulling back, Rusk opened one of the cans of powder, and careful to keep low, poured a quantity of the grains into a central pile. Then, moving slowly, he laid a powder string for a distance of five strides or so to his left, terminating it in the still half filled can itself, which he wedged deep in a clump of rotting saltbush.

Doubling back, he followed a like procedure to his right, doing it all with great caution, making certain there were no gaps in the line of poured powder. Finished, he returned to the starting point. He had now arranged two points of explosion, approximately twenty feet apart, with powder train fuses of equal length leading to each.

Crouched above the center mound, he dug into his pocket for a match, took a moment to glance around, see that no one had slipped up unnoticed, and then shielding the lucifer, scraped it against his boot heel.

The powder flared at first touch of the flame, sent up a tiny puff of smoke. The fuse trains caught from the mound, began to speed toward the half buried cans. Waiting no longer, Rusk wheeled, and again hunched low, ran back down the shallow draw.

He barely gained the trees when the explosions rocked the night, the one to his left going off with a tremendous roar and flash a breath or two before the one on the right. A blast of air struck Rusk forcefully, staggered him, and for a space of time he was caught in a weird, orange-colored world of swishing trees, of thundering echoes and swirling heat. And then again he was hurrying on. Far over to his left he could hear men shouting but all was suddenly drowned by a dull thudding as the frightened cattle sprang into wild flight.

Running along the edge of the grove Matt reached the point where he could see into the swale. Sutter's herd was a dark, shifting mass in the lurid light, flowing north. The explosions had worked just as he'd planned; the steers were racing away from the source of the blast where flames now were leaping high as they consumed the dry brush.

He could see riders wheeling in and out of the dark shadows, foregoing their original purpose of watching for him, turning now to the business of keeping the stampede more or less under control by endeavoring to guide the rushing cattle on a generally northern course.

He grinned into the night. He'd promised Frank Sutter he'd move off the herd—and he had. It made him feel good to defeat a man like him, prove to him he was not as big, as invincible as he fancied. Perhaps the rancher would now assume a reasonable stance, leave the Jackmans alone. But he'd hoped that hope before and nothing had come of it.

A horse plunged out of the trees, hard on his right. Rusk halted, flung himself to one side as the rider, a shrill yell on his lips, veered directly at him. Fire spurted from the pistol in the man's hand. Matt felt the bullet brush against his sleeve, and an instant later was going over when the oncoming horse struck him a glancing blow as it plunged by.

He went down hard, breath exploding from his mouth. Small lights danced before his eyes and vaguely he heard a voice—Monte Fox's voice, sing out.

"Over here! I got the bastard—over here!"

A grimness swept Matt Rusk. Shaking his head savagely, and ignoring pain, he rolled off into the brush, caught at a stout shrub and drew himself upright. Fox was wheeling about somewhere in the dark, preparing to come in again. Matt lurched to one side, still fighting the haze that shrouded his brain, tried to see into the trees . . . The chestnut should be close—just ahead. But that wouldn't help much—getting to the gelding; Fox was armed, and his yell would bring others. They'd never let him ride out of the grove alive.

Hunched low, he ran forward. The quick pound

of hooves behind him told him Fox had rushed in, believing him to still be there, lying on the ground, stunned.

"Not yet, damn you," he mumbled, hurdling a low clump of bushes.

Instantly a pistol cracked, splitting the night, setting up a new string of echoes . . . Another of Sutter's men, off to his right . . . He'd blundered straight into him. Now he had two of them to contend with.

Veering toward a thick trunked cottonwood, he paused as the rider, weapon raised as a club, closed in. Instinctively Matt threw himself flat. He felt the ground tremble as the horse thundered by no more than an arm's length away.

"Bruner!"

It was Monte Fox again . . . And Bruner—he'd been the one who'd stripped off his gloves while the others held him down in Jackman's yard.

Rusk jerked himself upright, plunged on. The chestnut was still his best bet; if he could reach him, lead him quietly off to the side, there might be a chance of slipping out of the grove unnoticed.

"He's in here!" Bruner shouted.

"Where the hell's—in here?"

"This way—"

Bruner had pivoted, was doubling back. He was a dark silhouette, arm again lifted to strike, coming in fast. But he had momentarily lost sight of his intended victim and was now looking about uncertainly. Rusk ducked low in the shadows, waited, abandoning all thoughts of finding the chestnut which he'd apparently overrun in the confusion.

Brunner swung in, face a hard, set circle in the weak light, drew abreast. Matt lunged from the darkness, caught the rider by the arm. Bruner cursed, came spilling out of the saddle, and locked together they went down into the brush.

"Bruner?"

Ignoring the apparent close-by presence of Fox, Rusk struggled to his feet, hand still gripping Bruner's arm. Dragging the rider half erect, he slammed him hard on the jaw with the heel of his free hand. Bruner grunted, went limp, pistol dropping from nerveless fingers.

Rusk pulled back, not sure of Monte Fox's position. He caught sight of the puncher at almost the same instant that he saw the chestnut. The gelding was in a small circle of cleared ground to his right, and a quick rush of sound very close to it told him Fox had also seen the horse, had cut back, knowing that he would be endeavoring to reach the animal.

Matt darted into the shadows, stepping over Bruner as he did, dropped behind a clump of prickly gooseberry bushes. An instant later Fox's horse, saddle empty, broke into the clearing where the chestnut was tied. At once Rusk changed positions; Fox was on foot now, stalking him.

Low, he waited at the edge of the open ground, ears straining to pick up any sound that would reveal Fox's whereabouts. A bush swished quietly—off to his left. Still crouched, he took a step backward, retreating deeper into the shadows. He felt the solidness of Bruner's dropped pistol under his foot. Impulsively, he reached down, scooped it up, holding it with both hands.

At that moment Monte Fox stepped into view, no more than a stride away. The puncher froze. The pistol held ready and level in his hand, lowered as his mouth gaped.

"Don't shoot!" he yelled.

Matt Rusk looked down at the weapon he was holding as if realizing its presence for the first time. Suddenly he threw it aside, off into the brush. He lunged at Fox, caught the pistol the puncher was gripping loosely. Wrenching it free, he sent it hurtling off into the darkness after Bruner's.

Seizing Fox around the waist, he whirled the man about. His heel came up against something half-buried, and he almost went down, losing his grasp of the puncher who did fall. Off-balance, Rusk staggered back. Fox was up immediately, lashing out with a booted foot. The blow took Matt in the crotch, sent pain rocketing through him in a blinding sheet. He buckled, threw out his arms to grapple with Fox as the man rushed in.

They went down in a twisting, flailing heap, Fox bearing the brunt of Rusk's weight. He gasped as Matt hammered a blow to his head, groaned as another smashed hard into his jaw. Rusk pulled himself to his knees, then succeeded in coming fully upright, one hand still clutching Fox's shirt front. Bruner nearby, was stirring slightly, rubbing dazedly at his eyes. Tightening his grip on Fox, Matt half lifted the man, threw him into Bruner. Both yelled as they went sprawling.

Rusk, a towering rage still swaying him, stepped in, took up a position near the two punchers. He waited until they had disentangled themselves, then said, "Get up!"

The men came to their feet slowly, each watching Rusk carefully, ready to jerk out of reach should he raise an arm to strike again.

"Start moving," Rusk said in a low, grinding tone. "Want you off Jackman land—fast. And tell Sutter next time I find his cattle around, I'll start a slaughter, not just a stampede. That clear?"

Bruner said nothing. Monte Fox nodded woodenly. Matt stared at them coldly. "Say it!"

"It's clear," Fox mumbled.

"The hell with you—" Bruner began in a sudden show of courage, and then jumped back as Rusk's leather covered fist swung for his jaw. He recovered, lowered his head. "All right—I hear you."

"Then get the hell out of here!"

Both punchers wheeled at once, struck off through the brush for their horses. Rusk, trembling, holding a tight rein on himself, crossed to where the chestnut was tied. Freeing him, he swung to the saddle.

He should go, too—get clean out of the country—wash his hands of the whole mess! He was not fooling anybody; he didn't have it anymore—just as he'd known all along. And he never would again. He'd proven that to himself when he picked up Bruner's gun . . . They'd intended to kill him, would, too, if they had gotten the chance. He knew that but he still couldn't make himself use the weapon.

He couldn't run out. He couldn't just disappear, leave April and Clint hanging there, wondering. He'd go back, but he'd make it plain to them that he was far from the man they thought, or hoped him to be.

# CHAPTER NINETEEN

Frank Sutter was slumped in his barrel leather chair on the porch when he heard what he thought was the last of the riders come in . . . Monte Fox and Dave Bruner. They'd more or less been in charge of things. They'd be the ones who could tell him what had happened.

Alone in the darkness, a cold cigar butt clenched between his teeth, he waited for the punchers to report. He already had the details on the stampede—it had cost him a dozen steers—what he wanted now was to hear that there'd be no more trouble from that goddam drifter who'd bedded down at Jackmans'. A couple of the other punchers had heard shooting over where Monte and Bruner had been hiding; they figured the two had cornered Rusk, nailed him for sure.

Sutter was not so confident. A self-contained, bitterly solitary man, he was finding it difficult to understand why things continually went wrong where Matt Rusk was concerned . . . One lousy saddlebum—a cripple at that—and he was upsetting a way of life that had run smoothly—if rough-shod—for years . . . How the hell do you figure a thing like that?

Take the plans he had for the Jackman ranch. It

wasn't that the girl and her brother had decided all of a sudden to bow their backs. Matters had been working out just as he'd planned; the place had been slow but sure going to hell, falling apart, and things were getting tighter and tighter for the Jackmans. It wouldn't have been long before they reached the point where they'd been forced to turn loose—and then this goddam Rusk blows in, screws up everything.

Frustration ripped through Sutter in a sudden gust. Pulling himself out of the chair in a quick, lunging motion, he came to his feet, snatched the butt from his lips and hurled it into the dark.

"Monte!" he shouted in exasperation. "Where the hell are you?"

"Ain't here yet, Mr. Sutter," a reply came from near the bunkhouse.

"Ain't here—goddammit I heard him and Bruner ride in!"

"Was Lafe and Civerolo."

Sutter swore deeply, dug into his breast pocket for a fresh cigar. "Want to see Monte soon's he shows up," he growled, and settled back in his chair.

He was tired. It had been a hard day—and then this goddam thing with Rusk had backfired, leastwise far as the cattle were concerned. He'd figured they'd have no trouble dabbing a few loops around Rusk when he showed up to drive off the herd; instead the bastard had managed to sneak in somehow, plant some charges of blasting powder, and set off a couple of explosions that not only got a dozen or so steers trampled to death but probably run ten pounds of tallow off all the rest.

Well, he'd taken all he was going to from this Rusk. Owed him plenty—for that business there in the Jackman yard when that fool girl had put a bullet in his hat—for that little yakking session there in town where Rusk had made him sort of look like a fool in front of everybody—not that it amounted to a damn. Nobody would ever have the guts to even mention it . . . And now this stampede. Wouldn't take long for word to get around that Rusk had carried out his threat and moved that herd.

But he wouldn't be crowing about it for long. Things could change mighty fast, and they were going to, Sutter thought, savagely biting off the end of the fresh cigar and spewing it into the yard; if Fox and Bruner hadn't already got the job done—then, by God, he'd hitch up the whole bunch and they'd go after . . .

"Mr. Sutter?"

It was Monte Fox. Sutter came up straight. "Took you long enough."

"Got here soon's I could."

"What about the drifter?"

Monte Fox moved to the edge of the porch. He pulled off his hat, rubbed at the back of his neck.

"Got away from us, Mr. Sutter. From Dave and me."

"Got away!" the rancher shouted, again vaulting erect. "How the hell could a cripple like him get away? Was told the pair of you had him cornered."

"Reckon we did—leastwise we thought we did. Had him, boxed off from his horse, but—"

"But he got away from two of you . . . Beats hell out of me how a jasper like him could sneak in under the noses of a dozen grown men, set off some gunpowder—and nobody able to do a thing about it . . . Then you show up, tell me you and Bruner box him in—only he got away. He put a bullet in you and Bruner—or something?"

"Nope. Just got to us before I could use my iron."

"Got to you—what's that mean?"

"Well, he yanked Bruner off his horse, knocked him cold. I tried slipping up on him, bumped right into him holding Dave's gun—and me holding mine . . . Next thing I knew he grabbed me, rassled me around some and threw me at Bruner—"

"You mean you come head on to him, both holding guns, and you didn't shoot?"

"Was him having the drop on me. I didn't get—" Sutter took a step nearer the puncher. "Why didn't he shoot then? What you'd expect a man to do."

"Beats me, too. Figured I was a goner there for a second, then he just ups and throws the gun away, grabs me. After it was all over ordered Dave and me to get moving. Said to tell you next time he'd do worse than just scare off your herd."

Frank Sutter was only half-listening. Something was breaking through to him, registering on his mind. Matt Rusk was a tough *hombre* with plenty of guts, but it was suddenly clear that he had no use for a gun—and that aversion undoubtedly was connected with his bunged-up hands. That, logically, led to another conclusion; Matt Rusk would never fight a man with a pistol, or any other firearm; the solution therefore when it came to coping with him was to stay out of his reach—and shoot.

Frank Sutter settled back in his chair. He had the answer now; everything was figured out. He drew a match, fired it with a thumbnail, sucked the cigar into life. Tossing the sliver of wood aside, he studied the glowing tip of the weed, a small, red eye in the darkness.

"Well, don't feel too bad about losing him, Monte," he said after a bit. "Got him straight now. He's plumb yellow when it comes to guns. It's that simple."

Monte Fox rubbed at his neck again. "You know, I was wondering about that. Why didn't he plug me back there when he had me cold? Then I got to thinking on the way over here that maybe he didn't have what it takes."

"Just exactly the answer. You figured he had the drop on you, but you could have gone right ahead, pulled the trigger on your iron and he'd a never done a thing."

"Never figured him for having a yellow streak—"

"Don't . . . He's only got one when it comes to using guns. Ain't nothing wrong with him otherwise—he'd take on a half a dozen of you with his bare hands and probably come out on top . . . So thing to do is keep out of his way— and don't back off using your own gun."

Monte Fox nodded slowly. "That mean you want me to go after him—"

"No, got other plans now. Tired of things hanging fire the way they are—and we've got a sort of natural to blame with this Rusk hanging around the Jackman place. They're going to have a real bad fire."

Fox said nothing, waited for the rest of it.

"Going to be sad, but both the Jackmans and that drifter'll be caught inside the house when it goes up. Probably was the drifter, being real careless about his smoking, that caused it."

Monte's face was sober. "You mean we're just going to get them trapped inside, then set fire to the place?"

Sutter contemplated the glowing tip of his cigar

again. "Like I said, it'll be a terrible, terrible accident. Only me and you and Bruner and—and, well, let's say Roscoe, will know how it started."

Fox stared off into the night. He was a bit mystified by Frank Sutter; never before had the rancher taken the trouble to cover over his tracks, or do anything on the sly. Always he'd just gone ahead, rode right down the middle of the trail and if anybody got in the way—bam, that was it! Didn't make a good goddam who knew about what he'd done or how—he was Frank Sutter and nobody better step up and ask any questions . . . But this Matt Rusk seemed to have changed his thinking for him—and his way of doing things.

"I ain't so sure about that," he murmured . . . That was another first, too; never before had he questioned Sutter when told to do something . . . "Burning folks up—a girl and a kid, 'specially—"

Sutter grunted. "Suit yourself. Got a dozen men just sweating to step in that easy job of yours—and some of them'll work for half the money I'm paying you . . . What the hell's got into you so goddam sudden? Getting soft-hearted?"

"No, only—a gal and a kid—"

"Don't think about that, just think how it could just as easy be an accident—without no help from us. It happens every day. Some ranch or some homesteader's place catches on fire, burns to the ground. Usually a bunch of kids and womenfolk caught in it."

"Guess you're right. Was letting my head wander a bit."

"Figured you'd wake up. Don't pay to get soft-hearted about anything, Monte. Man just plain cheats hisself when he does."

"Sure, Mr. Sutter . . ."

"Now, I'll meet you and the others in the kitchen at, say, about four o'clock—you, Dave Bruner, and Roscoe. Tell them to keep their traps shut—not that I give a damn what folks think but I'd sort of like to make this look like a real accident—genuine. See?"

Monte Fox nodded.

"We'll ride over there, wind this thing up and then go on in to town. We get there I'll pass the word along that we seen smoke coming from the direction of the Jackman place when we was riding down the valley, and maybe somebody ought to ride out see if everything's all right . . . You boys won't need to do no talking, just sort of fool around like you do when you go to town."

"Sure . . . Can say we seen the smoke, too."

"That's right. We didn't ride over there, we just seen the smoke . . . Now, expect you'd better go get yourself a couple, three hours sleep. Four o'clock comes along pretty early . . . Good night."

" 'Night, Mr. Sutter . . ."

# CHAPTER TWENTY

It was not far from midnight when Rusk rode into Jackman's yard. April and the boy were waiting for him, and as he pulled up to the front corral, both came off the porch to greet him.

"Matt—you all right?" April's question was anxious, fearful.

"All right," he answered in a subdued voice, and swung down.

Clint, grinning broadly, came in close and took the chestnut's reins. "I'll put him away for you . . . You drive old Sutter's cows off our range?"

"They're gone," Rusk replied.

The boy's smile widened even more, and turning he started for the barn with the gelding in tow. April laid her hand on Matt's arm.

"You look tired. Come sit on the porch for a few minutes . . . I've kept the coffee hot."

Rusk nodded, trailed her to the gallery and settled down heavily on its edge. April disappeared inside, returned quickly with a cup of steaming, black liquid.

He took it from her, holding it in the hollow of his two hands, swallowed several mouthfuls. "Obliged," he said. "Goes good."

She studied him for a moment, then: "Was there trouble?"

"Some. Ran into Monte Fox and that puncher they called Bruner. Sutter had men scattered all around the herd, just waiting."

"We heard the explosions. I didn't know what they were. Clint told me."

"Guess it caught them flat-footed."

He was deeply withdrawn, disturbed more than ever, April saw; his answers and statements were purely polite responses to her desire for information and not a free-hearted narration of the incident. Again silent, she considered him in the pale light, uncertain whether she should let him be, or talk, press him to open up, unburden his mind and rid himself of whatever it was harrying him.

The coffee seemed to help. He looked toward the barn. "Late for the boy to be up. Shouldn't have waited for me."

April smiled wryly. "I couldn't have made him go to bed if I'd tried. Had to see you when you got back—the same as I."

Clint crossed the yard, halted before Rusk and squatted on his heels. Picking up a twig he traced designs in the dust, endeavoring to mask the curiosity and excitement that gripped him.

"Sutter's old cattle—I'll bet they really took off flying when you set off that blasting powder!"

Matt nodded. "You'd win that bet. Ran straight back onto Sutter's own range . . . Makes me think of something. He may get some ideas of his own about stampeding your herd. First thing in the morning we'll drift your stock in closer to the house . . . Little pasture just south of here ought to do fine. Can keep an eye on them there."

"Ain't no water," Clint said.

"They can get by for a few days. We have to, we can drive them to the nearest hole, let them drink, then bring them back."

Matt tipped the cup to his lips, drained the last of the coffee. He had broken the deep reserve into which he had lapsed, apparently making an effort for the sake of the boy. April reached for the empty cup.

"There's plenty more."

He shook his head. "One's just enough."

The girl turned then to Clint. "Time you were in bed."

His face clouded instantly. "But I want to hear more about the stampede!"

"You've heard," Rusk said. "Nothing much to it. The powder went off—the herd jumped up and ran. Expect Sutter lost a few head."

"Didn't him and his bunch try to stop you or anything like that?"

"Didn't see me until the cattle stampeded, and then most of them got so busy looking after the steers they didn't have time for anything else . . . Now, you best get some sleep, boy. We got us a hard job ahead in the morning, moving your herd."

Clint got to his feet reluctantly, stepped up onto the porch, and with dragging steps disappeared into the house.

April took the empty coffee cup from Matt's hands, set it aside. She glanced toward the door, waited until she was certain the boy was in his room, and then brought her attention back to Rusk.

"There's more to it than you've told Clint, isn't there, Matt? I know from the way you sort of forced yourself to speak to him . . . I don't want to pry, but if you'd like to talk, I'm ready to listen."

"Not much more than what I've said," he replied, bringing his palms together, and beginning to scrub them gently. "This Bruner—and Monte Fox. There was a fight—a pretty good one.

"I picked up Bruner's pistol after I knocked him out—came face to face with Fox. He had his gun up, ready to shoot me. Guess he thought I had the edge on him and let his hand drop. Good thing for me—I couldn't have pulled that trigger even if my life depended on it—which it would have if Monte hadn't figured wrong."

April frowned. "You mean you could have shot Monte, only you didn't . . . I don't see why you're so upset—"

He shook his head. "Was pure luck, Monte thinking I had the drop on him. If he'd figured the other way I'd be dead right now . . . Whole thing adds up to this—to what I've sort of known for a long time—I haven't got what it takes to kill a man anymore."

April moved to the edge of the porch, sat down beside him. She wanted to repeat, *anymore,* but it didn't seem the thing to do.

"There's nothing wrong in not wanting to kill," she said quietly.

"There is if it's the time and the place—and a man who needs killing . . . Or maybe a question of killing or getting killed."

"That what you've been running from all these years, Matt—the moment when that might happen?"

He nodded slowly. "That's it. And tonight out there when I looked at Monte Fox and held Bruner's gun in my hands—both hands—I knew I'd backed myself into a corner. I couldn't run. Wanted to, but couldn't. Then Monte settled it by giving in. Next time Monte might not give in— or it could be somebody else who won't drop his gun . . . Answer's always been to not let myself get into something where a thing like this can happen."

His voice trailed off. She waited a few moments, said, "You've stopped running, Matt. What took place tonight proves it."

"Not sure. For a bit, out there, I was of a mind to ride on, not come back. Then I knew I couldn't do that. But there's something you ought to know. Not smart for you and the boy to depend on me too much. I have to face Monte Fox or somebody like him again over a gun, I won't be able—"

"You don't know that for sure! Monte left the question unanswered for you because he backed down. You don't know for sure you can't . . . Matt, all this goes back to Montana, doesn't it?"

He moved his shoulders slightly. "Everything goes back to Montana . . . What I do, what I feel, how I live—if you can call the last five years of my life, living."

"Tell me about it. Maybe it'll help—and Matt, it's important to me that I know."

He cast a sidelong glance at her, frowned, spread his hands wide and stared at the scarred gloves. "A long story—and not a very pretty one."

"It being long makes no difference—and far as not being a pretty one—I've been living one like that, too, ever since Papa was murdered."

Rusk turned, dark face long and shadowed in the night. He was frowning again, seemingly at a loss as to how she could find anything in his past of interest. After a bit he resumed his position, eyes straight ahead, staring off into the distance. A horse stamped wearily in the barn. The chestnut, probably. Somewhere back in the trees an owl hooted.

"Came West in 'seventy-two, my wife, my

brother, and me. He was a bit older but we'd always been close."

Rusk paused, seemed to be thinking back, reliving some special time in his life, thus did not notice the start of surprise in April when he mentioned having a wife.

"Settled down in the Tongue River country, up Montana way. Was tough going but things worked out pretty well. In about four years I had a house, a few good outbuildings and my herd was up to a thousand head.

"About that time a man by the name of Groth moved in north of us. Bought up a couple of the neighbors, and passed along the word he was going into the cattle-raising business right. Intended to turn the whole country into one big ranch, he said—his.

"Had a lot of money, it was told, and I reckon it was the truth. Made it during the war supplying something or other to the Union Army. Anyway, he was out to own everything along the Tongue."

Matt drew out his cigarette makings, rolled himself a quirley . . . April stirred, said, "Groth sounds a little like Frank Sutter."

He nodded. "The same stripe. You run into them everywhere. I've found . . . He came to me, offered to buy me out. Turned him down. Oh, the price was fair enough—I just didn't want to give up my place. My wife loved it, and for the first time we had something that was ours, something solid and real that we'd built with our own hands and sweat . . . Brother felt the same.

"Groth didn't take kindly to being refused. Was easy to see he was a man used to having his own way—and my place was in the middle of the strip he was out to own. Guess I was like a thorn sticking him in the worst place. Well, he never gave up. Kept dropping by trying to get me to change my mind. I wouldn't, and after a while things began to happen.

"We'd find a few steers dead—shot. We had a bad grass fire, and a couple of line shacks went up in flames. A water hole got poisoned and I lost some horses—and always after something like that here would come Sam Groth in his fancy, red-wheeled buggy—I never saw him on a saddle—to renew his offer."

"Was he doing all those things—setting fires and killing cattle, and such. Was it him?"

"Was—not him personally, you understand, but he was having his men do it. There were about a half a dozen or so of them, all hard cases, he kept around to do chores like that. One that sort of headed up the bunch was named Canon, Sid Canon . . . Folks got to calling them Groth's Wrecking Crew, and that's just what they were.

"Things kept happening, but we managed to keep going even though losses were starting to cut the ground right out from under us. Then one day I came upon Canon and another of Groth's bunch setting fire to a stack of winter feed I'd put up. They didn't see me coming and rode off before I got there, heading in to town. I put the fire out and went after them.

"I found them in a saloon, called their hand on it. When Canon went for his pistol, I shot him— dead. Other man backed off and ran. It was a fair fight and there were plenty of witnesses, so nothing was said to me by the law about it. Canon went for his gun first, I was lucky enough to not miss with my bullet.

"But that stirred things up plenty with Groth. A lot more things started happening, and so one day I rode over to Hempstead, that was the town where the sheriff had an office—we only had a marshal in the settlement where we all traded— and told him my problems.

"He listened but he said there wasn't much he could do unless I had some proof, could actually catch Groth red-handed . . . Did say he'd ride over first chance he got and look into the matter, however. So I headed back home."

Matt Rusk's voice dropped to little more than a husky whisper. The palms of his hands came together, began to chafe, scuff, set up those faint, dry squeaks.

"I was too late . . . Everything was over . . . I heard shooting when I got close. It worried me, so I rode in fast. Groth's bunch—the Wrecking Crew, were raiding the place, riding around the yard, shooting at everything that moved. The dog—horses in the corral—even the chickens.

"My wife and brother were laying on the porch. Both dead. I guess they heard the bunch ride in, stepped out to see what they wanted . . . Later I found they'd been shot about a dozen times—each."

April's breath was coming in low, painful gasps. "It—it must have been terrible!" she murmured.

"I don't know what happened to me then—or maybe that's wrong. Maybe I do know. Went loco, I guess. Anyway, I pulled my rifle and started shooting. Killed five of them—there were seven in the bunch—before they could get out of the yard. Then I swung my horse around and rode to Groth's ranch. I called him out and shot him down where he stood in his own yard."

Rusk hesitated, dark, shadowed eyes riveted to his hands. He cleared his throat, said: "After that I went back home, carried my wife and brother into the house, put them on the bed. Then I just sat down. Couldn't seem to think—know what I ought to do next.

"Must've been an hour or maybe two, later, when I heard horses in the yard and went out. There were a couple of dozen men in the party—local citizens, ranchers, some of Groth's hired help—even the town marshal. Before I knew it they grabbed me, tied me with ropes. Then some of them held my hands to the edge of the horse trough while others smashed my fingers with their gun butts.

"I don't recollect caring much, or even feeling it, but I remember somebody saying they had to fix me so's I'd never kill another man. Then the marshal said it was maybe a good idea, that while I was within my rights, doing what I'd done, I oughtn't to be turned loose to use a gun ever again.

"I thought a lot about what they'd said—and done while my hands were healing up and decided that if that's what working and living and trying to do right all boils down to, then the hell with it . . . Soon as I could I pulled stakes, sort of drifted along, working whenever I needed to at whatever I could find. Made it a rule to not let anybody or anything ever grow to amount to much with me.

"When I ran into trouble or met with somebody stirring it up—like Frank Sutter—I'd turn my back and move on. Way it looked to me, man couldn't win against their kind even when he was in the right. About all he could do was get the worst of it. Had proved that myself with Groth and his bunch—an all those good citizens and that marshal from a town in Montana."

"But you helped us," April said. "You didn't turn your back."

He shook his head. "Can't explain that myself. Tried to but nothing makes sense. Just sort of happened—and maybe it has something to do with the boy—and you. Could be I'm looking for the son I never had when I see Clint. And you, well—the woman I loved—lost . . ."

His words faded. The chafing of his palms ceased. He took a deep breath. "Usually when something took place, like that day I went into town with Clint, I'd just move on, get out of the country before I got in deeper. That morning it didn't occur to me to do that. Fact is, I never seemed to realize what was going on until out there tonight when I found myself pointing that pistol at Monte Fox and it came to me I couldn't pull the trigger."

"I'm glad," April said softly, unexpectedly. "I'm glad you couldn't."

He frowned, said impatiently. "Don't be. If Sutter pulls a raid, I'm not sure I can stand up and fight with a gun."

"Something we'll worry about if and when it happens. You didn't prove tonight that you haven't the courage to use a gun. I think you were simply proving to yourself that you're not a killer at heart the way those men in Montana made it look—and that you've been proving it to yourself all these years since.

"If the time comes when you're faced with the problem and there's no way out, then you'll know. . . . And I think you'll find that you will do what you have to do without really thinking about it."

Rusk shrugged. "Hope that'll be the way of it. Hate to let you and the boy down."

"Clint and I will take our chances," she said, and then added. "One thing, Matt, we don't want you to go. Not because of Frank Sutter and holding on to the ranch, things like that. He can have it all if that's what it'll take—but Clint worships you—and I—"

"Don't!" he said in a sharp, quick way, and then his manner softened. "April, there's nothing I can give you. I'm only half a man, full of doubts and uncertainties. There's just no way of knowing what's around the next corner for me—whether I'll die or be man enough to live."

"I know," she said softly, laying her hand upon his. At her touch of the leather there was no flinching, no tremor of horror on her part. It was as if the tortured flesh and battered bones masked by the impersonal leather were no different from any—from her own.

"I know," she said again. "You'll simply face whatever it is and act accordingly. You've stopped running from yourself—which is something nobody can do—and I'm glad that Clint and I were the ones to help you realize that."

Rusk did not look up. After a moment he said: "None of this makes a difference to you? What I've done—the fact that I'm a cripple—maybe even a coward?"

"Coward?" she echoed with a mocking laugh.

"How can you say that? The things you've done since you've been here; standing up to Sutter, to Henderson—the way you handled Charlie Heer and Monte Fox . . . And then, alone, driving off Sutter's herd . . . The last thing anyone will ever think of you is that you're a coward!"

"There's different kinds . . . A man can be afraid of himself."

"Only because he never stopped long enough to take a good look at himself—face up to all the things in the back of his mind that needed getting rid of. You've done that, Matt. You've put them out for good."

"I don't know," he murmured. "Tomorrow maybe I'll see things better. I'm tired—and right now nothing adds up."

April rose, smiling. "You'll see that I'm right. But I want you to know this, Matt; I—we—don't want to lose you. If you decide you have to move on—that it's the only answer, then Clint and I are going with you, if you'll have us . . . Good night."

Bending swiftly, she kissed him on the cheek, moved hurriedly on by, and entered the house.

Matt Rusk remained motionless for a long minute, his gaze on the starlight silvered slopes of the hills, and then pulling himself upright, he shrugged in a hopeless sort of way and headed for his bunk.

# CHAPTER TWENTY-ONE

"Matt! Matt!"

Rusk opened his eyes, sat up at the urgent cry and frantic tugging at his shoulder. It was still dark but pale light filtering in through the open window, falling across April's face revealed the anxiety that gripped her.

His first thoughts were of Sutter, that the rancher had struck back—but he would have heard, awakened. He threw his legs over the edge of the bunk, gripped her arms.

"What is it?"

"Clint—he's gone!"

Rusk stared at the girl. "Gone?"

April bobbed her head, brushed at her eyes. "Looked everywhere I can think of. I thought I heard something in the yard, got up to see what it was. There was nothing so I went back into the house. I stopped by his room, looked in—habit, I guess. His bed was empty."

"Had it been slept in?" Rusk asked, pulling on his boots. He was still partly dressed, having been so weary when he turned in that he had bothered to remove only his shirt and footgear.

"Yes—"

"Probably him you heard. Got a hunch where he'll be—with the cattle."

"Oh, I hope so—and I expect you'll be right. He feels he's not doing his part, that you're shouldering the work and taking the big risks."

"Only natural," Matt said, buttoning his shirt.

But the boy needed a good dressing down. It was foolish and dangerous for him to go off alone with the situation, insofar as Sutter was concerned, so touchy. He said nothing to April about it, however; there was no need to increase her alarm. If the boy wasn't with the herd then they'd have something to worry about. Wheeling, he snatched up his hat, hurried through the doorway and trotted to the barn, with April following closely.

"Buckskin's gone," he said, starting to saddle the chestnut. "Good sign he'll be with the herd. Could be he took it on himself to start moving the stock—remember saying last night we ought to bring them in closer. Expect he wanted to spare me the job, show he could help, too."

April nodded, seemingly reluctant to speak for fear of breaking down. That she was hoping desperately for Matt's hunch to be true and Clint would be found with the cattle, was apparent.

Finished with his gear, Rusk backed the gelding into the runway and swung onto the saddle. "Want you back inside the house," he said, looking down at the girl. "I'll find him . . . If I'm not back shortly, you'll know the two of us are driving the herd in."

He spurred away abruptly, leaving her there in the doorway, more disturbed than he wanted to admit. He glanced to the east. First light was laying a pale gray against the sky, creating a vast fan upon which the horizon was blackly etched. It wasn't as early as he had first thought; seemed he'd just stretched out, closed his eyes when April awakened him. He guessed he'd gotten four, maybe five hours sleep at that . . . Plenty for any man.

The chestnut loped on at a good clip in the morning freshness. Birds were beginning to stir and once a cottontail rabbit scampered across the gelding's path, fleeing in a wide curve that eventually led to dense brush.

He topped out the last roll of land, broke into the swale where he had earlier seen the herd. The cattle were on their feet, moving sluggishly eastward. Matt saw Clint then, and relief swept through him . . . The boy was astride his buckskin, a length of rope in his hand, cutting back and forth behind the cattle, slapping at them with his lash—and having a hard time getting the stubborn animals underway.

Matt grinned in spite of the situation and the possible seriousness it could have assumed; Clint was determined to pull his share of the load—and he certainly wasn't afraid of work. One boy attempting to drive two hundred contrary, cantankerous steers in the half dark! He'd find it hard to chide him particularly since he was doing it to lighten the load he felt was being assumed unequally.

Spurring the chestnut down the slight grade, he shook out his rope, arranged a manageable length, and cut in beside the boy.

"Use some help?" he yelled, slapping at a lagging steer.

The tautness left the boy's face at once. He grinned. "Sure can! Critters sure hate being moved out of here."

"Can't blame them," Matt answered. "Been easy living."

But with the two of them working steadily, they soon had the drive underway, and the herd shaped up into a fairly tight wedge moving along at normal pace in the early light. Rusk then drew in near Clint, looked close at the boy.

"Gave your sister quite a scare—me, too—leaving the way you did."

Clint dropped his glance. Rusk drew out his tobacco and paper, twirled a smoke. "Should've woke me . . . Too big a job for one man."

The smile came back to the boy's face at the straight, man to man attitude. He shook his head. "You were dog tired, could see that last night. Figured you ought to get some sleep. Only right I was taking on more of the real hard work, anyway."

"Won't argue with that. One thing—we had

215

a deal. Idea was to never take chances—like leaving April alone. She's by herself right now."

"Know that—but you were there when I left."

Matt shrugged. Clint was reversing things, and to his young mind it was logic, made sense. What he was failing to consider was the danger he placed himself in when he left the premises.

"We'll hash it over later," Rusk said. "Once a deal's made, a man's got to stand by it, else he's going to cause trouble."

He pulled away then, swinging around the end of the herd, loping in alongside its flank. He was thinking of his own words—that April was alone; perhaps one of them should return to the ranch. They weren't too far from the small valley where he had planned to graze the stock, but it would take four, perhaps five hours to make the drive. He'd stay with Clint a bit longer, until they were beyond the ridge and almost in sight of the house, then he'd return to the ranch. . . .

Sunrise was at hand, with long, golden fingers soaring into the sky, washing away the gray, spreading a soft radiance over the hills and flats. Turning about, Rusk doubled back, aware of the changing light, the fading shadows, the complete and utter beauty of the sun's first rays, soft as thistle down in those first early moments. There was something special about this particular morning; Matt Rusk was aware of that fact, unaware of the reason.

It came to him abruptly, breaking through the self imposed barriers in his mind, as the sun itself pushed up above the rim of hills to the east; it was April Jackman—and the boy, Clint . . . They were making it different. They had somehow changed him—now were changing all else for him, making him conscious of the things he'd once known and appreciated—but forgotten. As had the biblical Lazarus . . .

Rusk halted, frowning. Fear suddenly gripped him, tightened his throat. A faint popping sound had reached him, and well above the tree tops to the east, a boil of ugly, black smoke was surging upward. It was in the direction of the ranch.

April!

It was the first thought to seize his mind. Sutter had struck. April was alone. He rowled the chestnut cruelly, whirled him about on hind legs, sent him springing ahead, racing for the trees.

Behind him he heard Clint yell. Glancing over his shoulder he saw the boy had noticed the smoke, too, was coming. Matt raised an arm, waved him back; if Sutter's men were still there, he'd best not be around; he'd only serve to complicate matters.

Rusk reached the barn, curved in behind it. The first thing he saw was the wall of flames that claimed the rear of the house. Fear once again rolled through him. April—where was April? A gunshot flatted above the crackling fire. A rider trotted across the yard, having trouble holding his horse . . . Monte Fox . . .

The puncher had a pistol in his hand. He raised it, planted a bullet in the closed door of the Jackman kitchen. Rusk saw other men then—one at the north end of the house, another to the south. Understanding came to him. April was trapped inside the structure; they were keeping her pinned down by shooting at the doors and windows, thus preventing an escape.

An oath ripped from Rusk's lips. An impulse to spur the gelding, race into the yard, knock Monte Fox off his horse—and all the others, too—possessed him. And as quickly the foolhardiness of such a move occurred to him. Get April out—that was the urgent need; then settle with Frank Sutter's men.

Dropping from the chestnut, he ducked low, and in the now thick smoke hanging over the yard, skirted the outbuildings and made his way to the south end of the house. The dim outline of a rider sitting his horse just a few yards from the window brought him up short. That part of the house had not yet begun to burn, but tongues of flame were beginning to lick hungrily at the corner.

Rusk catfooted silently in behind the man on the horse. He couldn't see the puncher too well in the smokey haze, but he didn't appear to be one of Sutter's men he'd met before. It made no difference. Rising suddenly out of the brush, Matt seized the man by the arm, jerked him from the saddle, slammed him to the ground. The puncher yelled, tried to draw the pistol at his hip. Rusk smashed him into unconsciousness with a murderous blow to the jaw.

Leaping over the man, he darted to the end of the house, halted at the window. It was Clint's room. Picking up a short piece of wood, he broke the glass, reached in, tried to turn back the latch. His fingers failed to manipulate the small, narrow lever, and in a burst of temper, he gripped the framework, tore it out and flung it aside.

Heaving himself into the opening, he hung, half way, shouted: "April!"

No answer came. Again a terrible fear clawed at him. Throwing himself into the room, thick with choking smoke and trapped heat, he hurried into the short hallway.

"April!"

He did not wait for an answer—one that did not come, but moved deeper into the house, gagging, eyes smarting, every breath a stabbing pain . . . She was not in the room she ordinarily occupied. He made his way to the quarters that had been her father's . . . He recalled telling her that in event of trouble, she was to stay either there or in the kitchen . . . She'd not be in the latter—not with the walls burning furiously and smoke hanging in heated layers so dense as to be impenetrable . . . He kicked the connecting door shut, closed off that area, staggered into the bedroom. He saw her at once, lying on the floor.

Bending down, he scooped her into his arms, started back along the hallway. The haze was thickening there now and he could scarcely see with his watering, stinging eyes. He could feel the searing heat from the roaring flames of the west wall as they gathered strength, sought to envelop the entire roof and south end of the structure.

He reached Clint's room, made it across to the window, April limp but gasping and choking. Pushing her through the opening, he lowered her to the ground, crawled after her, lay quiet beside her for several moments. Fire was taking over the entire structure now . . . If he had been five minutes later . . .

Rising, he took her in his arms again, moved off into the popping, smoking brush. April stirred, looked up at him. Wild fear leaped into her eyes, and then followed relief as she recognized him. A sob tore at her throat.

"Oh, Matt—I prayed you'd come!"

Her words broke off suddenly as a spasm of coughing seized her. He held her close, having his own trouble with the smoke in his lungs, but he carried her easily as he would a small child as he circled behind the lesser buildings, heading for the barn and the place where he'd left the chestnut.

Sutter's men were still in the yard, moving about in the dense pall of smoke, apparently still thinking April, and he guessed Clint as well as he, were trapped inside. The man he'd knocked from the saddle, was as yet unmissed.

"Put me down, Matt . . . I can walk—I'm all right."

At her insistence Rusk placed the girl on her feet. She clung to him briefly, unsteadily, and then together they continued.

"I tried to get out when they set fire to the house," she murmured in a distraught voice. "Every time I went to a door or window—somebody would shoot, drive me back."

With April out of the house and that terrible fear behind him, the sullen throb of hate for Sutter and his men once more forged to the surface, became increasingly intense at this example of the rancher's ruthless mind.

"You see Frank Sutter?"

April nodded, her face barely visible in the haze. "He's there . . . And so's Monte Fox and Dave Bruner—and some other man I didn't recognize . . . Saw them all. Matt, what about Clint? Was he all right?"

"Was moving the herd, like I thought. Told him to stay back. Afraid he might get hurt here . . . Not sure that he did."

April stiffened. Her fingers clutched at Matt's arm. "Maybe—if he followed—"

Suddenly taut, Rusk pushed out ahead of the girl, made his way to the opposite corner of the corral along which they were moving. Halting there, he crouched, peered into the yard, tried to see through the heavy fog. He spotted a rider, vague and indistinct off to his right; another, sitting idly on his saddle at the north end of the yard, looked like Sutter.

"Matt!"

April's voice was an anguished gasp. He pivoted to her, followed her pointing finger. Clint, a crumpled shape in the murky gloom, lay face down in the dust near the barn.

# CHAPTER TWENTY-TWO

Instantly Matt Rusk leaped away from the corral, legged it for the slight form. Somewhere near the front of the house a man was yelling but he didn't listen, made no effort to understand the words. He reached the boy, knelt beside him, slipped his thick arms under the small body.

April, crowded against him. "Is—is he—" she began in a breathless, stifled way and stopped.

"He's alive," Matt said, rising. He paused, glanced around, started for the open doorway of the barn. Half there, he changed his mind; the bunkhouse would be better; not only would a bed be available, but there'd be water and clean rags, and there were a few medicines, accumulated over the years by the hired hands, on a corner shelf.

Running in long, jerky strides, the boy cradled against him, Rusk rounded the back corner of the barn, crossed behind it, came finally to the rear of the bunkhouse. The door was closed. April, panting from her efforts to keep up with Rusk, breath further shortened by fear and anxiety for her brother, pushed ahead of him, tried the knob. The panel was locked. An exclamation of impatience slipped from Matt's lips, and lifting a leg, he drove a booted foot against the door, blasted it open.

Stepping inside, he carried Clint to one of the bunks, gently placed him on the corn husk mattress. April, silent, tense, leaned over the boy, began to remove the blood-soaked shirt plastered to his torso. Her fingers were shaking but she did not falter at the task. Rusk, crossing the room, took up the bucket of water he had earlier set on the washstand and grabbed a handful of the clean towels April had provided, took all to her.

She had uncovered the wound. He examined it closely, grunted in relief. "Not too bad. Bullet went through his shoulder."

"He's lost a lot of blood," April murmured, dipping one of the towels in the bucket and wiping around the edges of the wound. "I'll fix a bandage . . ."

That would help some, Matt knew, but the boy needed the attention of Doc Haley as soon as possible. He glanced toward the yard. The fire was beginning to die, most of the main house having been consumed. Smoke yet hung in dense layers in the yard, shutting out the sunlight, and there was a hot, acrid smell to everything.

"Get the kid's body—throw it in there with the woman's."

Frank Sutter's harsh voice . . . April choked back a cry. "When they don't find him, they'll start hunting," she said fearfully. "They'll find us in here." She gave the back door a quick look. "If you'll carry Clint, we can go out that way, hide in the brush."

Rusk's face was a bleak mask . . . They could do that, all right—crouch in the weeds, play a sort of hide and seek game with Sutter and his men until they grew tired and rode off; he might even get a chance to reach his horse, and maybe Clint's buckskin, load April and the boy on them and start for town . . . And maybe young Clint Jackman would survive all the delay, and maybe he wouldn't.

"Hell, he ain't here!" Dave Bruner yelled from the barn. "Seen him fall—right there by that shed . . . Was laying there no more'n ten minutes ago. Gone now."

"Look inside the barn—that bunkhouse, too," Sutter called back. "Couldn't have got far, crawling . . . Goddammit, we're taking too much time! Still got to run down that drifter . . . Monte! Get over here and give Dave a hand!"

In that moment of crisis Matt Rusk stood on the brink of a depthless chasm, one that ran back over the years, all the way to Montana; one that could go on forever, even to infinity. He realized the time for decision was at hand, that he had reached a fork in the trail of his life and a choice must be made . . . He could face up to what he, as a man, should do or he could continue in the old, safe pattern, avoid trouble—run . . . April had made it easy for him by suggesting that very course herself.

He wheeled suddenly, snatched up the shotgun he'd placed near the window, grabbed a handful of shells.

"Stay down," he said to the girl in a quick, sharp way, "This won't take long." Crossing to the door he stepped out onto the landing.

"Sutter!" he yelled. "You won't have to hunt—I'm here!"

"It's the drifter!" Monte Fox, almost directly in front of Matt, yelled.

Rusk saw the puncher reach for his pistol. Holding the shotgun straight out, he jammed a rigid forefinger into the weapon's trigger guard, hauled back against the trigger itself. The gun roared. Monte Fox buckled into a smoking lump, went sideways off his saddle.

Pain stabbed into Rusk's leg and the crack of a pistol seemed almost in his ear. He staggered, pivoted, dragged his finger against the other curved trigger of the scattergun. The charge caught Dave Bruner coming in, slammed him into the dust.

Frank Sutter was yelling: "Get him! Get him! Kill the sonofabitch!"

Breaking the double, Rusk tipped the weapon up, emptied the chambers of the spent shells, fumbled in fresh ammunition as he backed toward the corner of the bunkhouse. He couldn't see Sutter—and there was another rider some-where—the one he'd knocked out earlier. He paused, favoring his leg, tried to locate the men.

Abruptly Sutter was before him. The rancher's pistol came up, spat fire. Matt heard the thud of the bullets driving into the wall of the bunkhouse behind him, coolly fired the shotgun from the hip. Sutter yelled, threw up both arms and fell from his horse.

He saw motion on the opposite side of the yard in that same instant, spun to face the fourth man. A harsh stream of hate was pouring through him as he swung the shotgun to bear upon the rider . . . Here before him in the yellow pall of Jackman's yard were all the Groths, the Sutters, the men of their kind with whom he'd had to contend. These were the vultures, the stealers—the killers of not only life but a man's soul as well—and retribution was his! Never again would any . . .

"Matt!"

April's scream was like a shaft of pure light slicing through the burning haze in his mind. He stood motionless, shotgun leveled at the fear-paralyzed man, forefinger stiff against the slender bit of curved metal that was the difference in life and death for the rider.

"Matt—don't!"

Slowly he lowered the weapon, aware now that the man had his arms raised, begging surrender. From the other side of the yard Frank Sutter stirred, groaned, but there was no sign of life in Monte Fox or Dave Bruner. He heard April come out onto the landing of the bunkhouse, heard her voice.

"You're hurt—"

He shook his head. It was nothing. He motioned at the rider with the barrel of the shotgun. "Throw down your pistol . . . Then get off that horse."

The man complied hastily. Rusk motioned toward the barn. "Spring wagon and team in there. Get them hitched together—quick. Got to get that boy you shot in to the doctor. He doesn't make it—you won't either."

"Your leg—" April said, taking him by the arm and trying to lead him into the bunkhouse.

He pulled away as if not hearing, walked slowly to where Frank Sutter lay. The rancher, one hand clutching at his shoulder, stared up at him. He was bleeding badly.

"You had enough?" Rusk demanded, his voice still taut, harsh. "I've learned how to kill again, Sutter. You made me learn—and I'm ready to go on if you—"

"Get me to town," the rancher said, shaking his head. "Need Haley—bad."

"Why should I? That boy in there you shot— the girl you thought was burning to death inside that house—they didn't mean anything to you. But they do to me so now it's my turn. I'm looking out for them—and letting you bleed away your stinking, greedy life. Be doing the world a favor—"

"Matt—the wagon's ready." April's voice broke through the angry mist that swirled about in his mind. "And Clint's all right. The bleeding's stopped."

He looked at her closely. The tightness had fled her face and she seemed more at ease, relieved. That seemed to give him release, also. He grinned, nodded. "That boy's plenty tough," he murmured with a note of pride. "He'll do fine."

He looked toward the bunkhouse where the rider was carrying Clint into the open, placing him on a mattress he'd already laid in the wagonbed. April had shifted her attention to Sutter.

"Is he hurt bad?"

"Few buckshot in the shoulder, maybe the chest. Not enough to kill him."

"We can put him in the wagon, beside Clint—"

Matt shook his head. "No, we won't bother. I'll send somebody back from town."

"But he'll die—bleed to death!"

"What difference it make? He's never thought twice about taking somebody's life—why should we bother? That's the trouble with people—they're too damn quick to forget, to overlook things—"

"There's such a thing as forgiveness, Matt—and that's important."

"Forgiving him is like forgiving a rattlesnake after he's bit you . . . He doesn't deserve it—not after what he's done to you and Clint."

"Maybe you're forgetting there's the law . . . I know you don't hold much with it, that you have no faith in justice—but it's there just the same . . . And we ought to keep Frank Sutter alive so's he can face up to it."

"He'll worm out of it, same as all the other—"

"Not this time. Even he's not big enough to hush this up because we've got a good witness." She pointed to Sutter's rider, leaning against the back wheel of the wagon.

Rusk looked off through the thinning smoke toward the low hills. Forgiveness . . . Law . . . Justice . . . He'd had no part of them for five long years, but it all sounded right, somehow, coming from April . . . In fact, everything had changed around, seemed right.

He motioned to the rider, pointed at Sutter. "Load your boss in, then head for town. We'll be right behind you."

Turning then, he walked to where the chestnut was tied, brought him and one of the loose horses—Bruner's he guessed it was—back to where April waited. The wagon began to roll out of the yard and Rusk helped the girl up to the saddle, climbed onto the chestnut, and swung around.

April, holding the reins lightly, had not stirred.

She was staring at the still smoldering shell of the house.

"Everything's gone, Matt," she said in a lost voice.

"Only a house and what was in it," he replied quietly. "And I reckon if a woman can help a man rebuild his life, then together they sure shouldn't have much trouble rebuilding a house."

Books are produced in the United States using U.S.-based materials

Books are printed using a revolutionary new process called THINKtech™ that lowers energy usage by 70% and increases overall quality

Books are durable and flexible because of Smyth-sewing

Paper is sourced using environmentally responsible foresting methods and the paper is acid-free

**Center Point Large Print**
600 Brooks Road / PO Box 1
Thorndike, ME 04986-0001 USA

**(207) 568-3717**

**US & Canada:**
1 800 929-9108
www.centerpointlargeprint.com